Frequency Seven

by

Albert Samuel Tukker

Copyright ©2006 ASTukker

ISBN 978-0-557-02472-8

Other works include:
"Gamer"
"StoneAge Wizard"
"Solitaire"
"From the Attic"

You can find more works by,
and information about
Albert S Tukker at:
http://AlbertSamuelTukker.com

Chapter I

He had been walking, head down, left thumb up and out when he noticed his shadow cast by the approaching headlights moving directly in front of him. For a moment he thought the vehicle wasn't going to stop and veered to his right. Then he heard gravel stopping rubber and weight. He turned to an older model pick-up, carrying a cab-high shell. It was waiting for him. He stepped to the passenger door and opened it.

Leaning in, the warmth of the pick-up truck flushed the hitchhiker's face. The icy drizzle and cold night air had chilled him throughout and he shivered as he climbed into the vehicle, placing his backpack between his feet.

"Thanks for the lift," the hitchhiker offered.

"Close the door," came the driver's curt reply.

The thump of the backpack on the floorboard awoke a sleeping spider under the seat. It moved to investigate. The two-inch spider had a long, golden-yellow abdomen and a white body with black patches near the edge where each leg connected. Long, pipe cleaner legs were the same golden-yellow of the abdomen, banded with thick, black hair at the joints, the small leg on the left side broken off near the body. It quickly crawled to the bag.

The driver looked in his side view mirror, then pulled away from the shoulder and back onto the interstate highway, shifting gears at the steering column.

They were headed west on Interstate 80, just a couple miles west of Cheyenne, Wyoming. Classical pipe organ music played from a CD player set in the dash. The glow from the dash illuminated the driver.

Somewhere in his late thirties and big boned, the driver had black hair that was cut short, with whitewalls over the ears, a beard that was full, neatly trimmed and as black as the hair on top. He wore a safari-like outfit; khaki pants with oversized pockets on the legs, and a khaki shirt with pockets on the sleeves and abdomen. "You headed for Laramie." The driver said, more of a hopeful command than a question.

The hitchhiker could feel the animosity from the driver. He turned from looking out the side window and spoke to the windshield. "Vegas. Or as far as you'll take me."

The driver didn't flinch. "I can take you as far as Laramie."

"That'd be great." The hitchhiker reached over and extended his right hand. "Names Andy. Thanks again for the ride."

The driver just looked at Andy's offer, then turned back to the windshield. "As far as Laramie."

Andy dropped his hand, turning back to the windshield himself and murmured, "Laramie will be fine."

Suddenly Andy didn't want the ride, not with the coldness of his host and the nausea that started when he closed the door. But, he was going to get warmed up before they reached Laramie. He bent forward and unlaced his boots, letting the warmth from the cab soak in. He then unbuttoned several layers of flannel shirts and rested his head against the side window. He was spent. Over the last two days he had slept six hours and walked fifty miles. He closed his eyes.

The driver glanced at his passenger. The front of Andy was soaked from the rain, his collar length hair straightened, strands stuck to his face and a week old beard. Layers of shirts and a pair of jeans were all he had to protect him from the elements. The hiking boots he wore were the only decent item for the weather. He cranked the windshield wipers up another notch.

"Where's your coat?" The driver bluntly asked, wanting to add, but didn't - 'You stupid sandmite.'

Andy raised his head off the window, drowsy from the warmth. "It was in my camper; stolen last week. All of my clothes, all my tools, gone."

"Well, it sure helped in you getting picked up just now. If you had had a coat, I would have kept on going. But I didn't have the heart to let you walk in the rain like that."

"Thanks," Andy muttered, feeling a bit guilty.

The driver then reached over and turned the music up a little.

Andy put his head back on the window, the nausea seeming to increase with the volume. Exhausted from the road, he didn't want to pry, nor bicker. He pushed sleep to escape his suddenly sick stomach.

Andy held on tightly to the thick, silky rope suspended vertically in a void. The void was filled with a fog, a cobweb grey in colour, infinite in depth. A hundred feet below him a web stretched across his vision, the strand in his grasp anchored in the center. The spider of the web, yellow and white and black and large, was off to one side passively watching him. Beneath the web was more fog. Above him was but more white rope that faded into the grey.

Andy climbed hand over hand up the opalesce dragline; he climbed for hours, he climbed through several heartbeats. When he thought he had climbed an eternity, arms aching, hands barely able to grasp the rope, he stopped and looked down. There was nothing but the single strand as far as he could see.

After catching his breath and regaining some feeling in his hands, Andy started to climb again, only to stop after one pull when the rope began to tremble. Andy closed his eyes and held on; legs entangled in the rope as it shook violently, bucking him like a wild horse.

When the movement stopped seconds later, Andy opened his eyes and looked around. Below him was the web and the spider. He closed his eyes again, hard, forcing tears to flow. Then a soft, feminine, determined voice whispered in his mind, "Let go".

Eyes still closed, Andy let go of the rope.

He plopped into a cushioned seat as if sitting down. When he opened his eyes he was in the passenger seat of a car, long and low. And it wasn't dark and raining outside, it was bright and sunny, and from the short shadows it was just past noon. Nor was he traveling down the freeway in Wyoming. He was on a dirt road in the middle of a desert. Tall ridges and mountains on the hazy horizon encircled him. Ahead, in the near distance, Andy could see a small, fuzzy building.

Then the driver spoke, a hollow voice peppered with the clicking of wood against wood. "This place is a secret. I don't know why I'm showing it to you."

Andy turned to the driver and blinked. It was the driver that had just picked him up in Wyoming, but he was wooden, a marionette.

"Name's Linus," the driver said. "I'm suppose to take you there." Linus nodded at the approaching building, then backward towards the rear of the car, "She says to."

The clicking Andy had heard was the puppets jaws slapping together. Silk strings, thin and white, were attached to the puppets joints. The strings led to the back window where a yellow and white spider, the size of a small boy, sat with two legs dangling over the back of the seat. The other five legs and the spinnerets were controlling the strings, the small leg on the left broken at the first joint and useless. Andy could see dust roll out behind the car as they sped onward. Then two eyes shifted from watching the puppet to Andy. "We will be there soon," Andy heard in his head. Again the voice was feminine, soft, soothing.

"Where?" Andy heard himself ask. Everything felt unreal, yet real. It was as if he and the world had been encased in a gelatin, or a thick cobweb.

Again the feminine voice spoke into the darkness behind his eyes, "Everything's going to be fine."

The tone caused Andy to relax. He watched the scenery go by as the puppet drove. The land was flat, the surrounding hills tens of miles away. Heat rippled the ground ahead of them, the fuzzy building focusing into a chain-link fence, twenty feet high. And there was something else, something tall. A radio tower.

Minutes later the puppet stopped the car near the fence. "Out", the soft voice of the spider commanded.

Andy got out of the car and shut the door, then watched as the puppet exited the car. The spider, normal size on the puppets shoulder, leapt to the roof as the door shut, keeping control of the strings. As the marionette rattled around the front of the car with noisy joints, the two-inch spider scurried across the roof of the car and onto Andy's shoulder.

Andy flinched, then apologized. "Sorry."

"Everything's going to be fine, Andrew," the spider whispered into his ear, it's minute breath cool on his skin. "Follow Linus."

As Andy followed the marionette the few yards to the fence, he asked the spider her name.

"Arabella," the spider whispered.

"How do you know my name?"

"I know everything about you."

Andy's eyes flicked to his left shoulder, then back. He stopped walking. They were at the fence, Linus almost touching it, Andy and Arabella several steps to the right of the puppet. The only sounds were the breeze brushing by their ears, the rattle of Linus fidgeting, and a lonely bird somewhere behind them calling to no one. Then a rumbling came from the other side of the fence, directly in front of them. The ground seemed to vibrate beneath his feet, in sympathy with the rumbling. Linus rattled a little louder.

"What's going on?" Andy asked.

Frequency Seven

Andy felt a slight movement on his shoulder, then Linus raised an arm and pointed to movement inside the fence. Andy followed the point and realized he was witnessing a missile silo opening its launch doors.

When three columns of white-grey smoke shot out of the ground from exhaust ports around the open doors, Andy thought he had gone deaf from the jet engine roar. Then Linus jerked and Andy heard the wooden joints rattle. He could also still hear the bird whistling behind them. There was simply no sound of the jet engine roar.

As flames licked at the smoke at the exhaust ports, the nose of the missile slowly rose above the ground. Still, Andy could not hear the engine noise. When the missile left the silo, a caressing wind and the fidgeting puppet was all Andy heard. He watched the silent missile disappear before saying anything.

"Is it an illusion?" Andy asked.

"No," Arabella whispered, then dropped the strings to the marionette and crawled into Andy's shirt pocket.

Linus turned to Andy when the strings touched the ground. He took the few steps to Andy and grabbed Andy firmly by the arm. "Wake up!" the hollow, clicking voice ordered. "Wake up!"

"Wake up. We're at a Rest Area." It was the driver, alive and in the flesh. The passenger door was open and he was shaking Andy awake.

The cold, outside air slapped Andy in the face. He was back. The rain had stopped and the night sky was clear and starry, but another front was on the way. "Hunh? Where?" he mumbled.

"We're at a Rest Area. Fifteen miles this side of Laramie," the driver looked to the freeway, then added, "walking distance. I thought you might like to use the can," he explained.

"I sure could," Andy replied. The driver backed away from the door.

Andy swung his legs out of the car and quickly tied the laces of his boots, his breath visible. The air was thick with pine. He buttoned an inner layer shirt as he stood, the blood rushing to his legs. He grabbed for the car door and held on until his head cleared.

"You okay?" The driver asked.

Andy thought he heard sincere concern, but realized it was annoyance when he looked at the driver. "Yeah, just a little lightheaded. Stood too fast." He stuck a hand in his pants pocket, rustling change. Then, because of the dream, he checked his breast pockets. "Maybe there's vending machines here."

"The sign said there was," the driver said coldly as he backed away a few steps. He watched as Andy headed for the building. He waited until Andy walked around the corner of the building, then walked back to his truck and left.

While Andy stood in front of a urinal, the dream flashed through his mind in clips. As he washed his hands he had a sense, a feeling, that the dream meant something. That he had been shown something. Let in on a secret.

He stuck his head under the electric hand dryer to dry his damp hair, oblivious to how long it was taking to freshen up. Visions of the dream and the spider filled his thoughts.

After leaving the restroom Andy went to the vending machines. From the caged dispensers he purchased a cup of coffee and a candy bar. As he rounded the brick building and into view of the parking lot, he stopped. The parking lot was empty, except for three eighteen wheelers, and his backpack on the sidewalk.

Chapter II

    Andy sat on the exhaust side of the soda machine, his back against the cage holding them captive. A flannel shirt draped over his bent legs, the backpack under his knees, he fiddled with his shirt collars, then rested his head on the bars. The dream in the truck was a foggy impression now, floating aimlessly through his mind as he waited for the weather to dry up. He had finished the cup of coffee an hour ago, and a can of soda a few minutes ago. Five cars had come and gone since he was abandoned. None had looked approachable. He contemplated going over and reading the maps and information displays again. If he hadn't caught a ride by sun up, he would start walking.

    He was not angry with the driver that had left him there. He was disappointed in the man, but couldn't blame the guy for being cautious in today's world. Andy conceded that he could be perceived as dangerous by looks alone. But Andy didn't really think the man was being cautious. Linus wanted his solitude.

    Besides, he didn't want to ride in that pick-up any longer anyway. The truck made him sick. He hadn't felt like throwing up since he stepped out of the cab. He did wish he had made it to Laramie, though.

Andy shifted his position, returning blood flow to one leg, cutting the circulation to another. A few moments later the caffeine took effect. He stood, stretched, then made a quick walk to the restroom. It had taken him three days to get here from Omaha and he felt that he had walked half the distance. The restroom was warm. He toyed with the idea of resting there for a moment, the warmth, the dry floor, the pungent odor. He quickly dismissed the idea as too dangerous, then headed back to the vending machines. He drifted in and out of a light sleep as he considered buying a bus ticket in Laramie, the next step up from hitchin'.

A bus ticket would mean dipping into his retirement fund though, savings he had accumulated since leaving his grandparents eleven years ago. Most of it was in investments, but taking money out other than for emergencies was difficult for him to do. Freezing to death wasn't going to do him any good, though. When he made it to Laramie, he would get a ticket. It couldn't be more than two hundred dollars. That won't hurt too much, and a warm bus with soft seats would feel wonderful.

Just as Andy was about to nod off into a dream of plush reclining seats, a vehicle entering the rest area brought him back to the cold Wyoming night. He grabbed his backpack on the way to his feet and limped towards the parking lot, one leg asleep.

A school bus, nine windows to a side, had pulled into the parking lot. The front, snout, of the bus was narrow with rounded corners. The colour was a faded blue-jean blue. The school name had been replaced with flowing, hand-painted, emerald-green words - *Glass Reality*. On top, from front to middle, was a luggage rack, stuffed tight with musical instruments, drums, and duffel bags. It looked to be tied down thoroughly. A round, metal smokestack stuck out of the roof at the rear, grey smoke streaming straight up. The side door swung open then, a thin veil of purple smoke escaping out the top of the doorway.

A tall, muscular man with a crew cut, wearing bell-bottom jeans and a tie-dyed tank top came down the steps. He stopped on the bottom step and looked around before heading for the back of the bus, slipping around it without a shudder.

Next down the steps was a shorter man, thinner build, with long, blond hair tied in a ponytail. He wore a heavy jacket, pulling it together as he followed the first man around the back of the bus.

In the open doorway Andy could see the driver of the bus rise and come to the door. The driver also had long, blond hair, but it was in dreadlocks that scraped his lower back. He grabbed a long coat and stepped off the bus, walking towards Andy. Glass Reality was a band. Punk rock, rock, garbage rock. Some kind of rock.

Andy, still sleepy, watched the tall, lanky stranger approach as if in a dream. The young driver swept into his canvas drover with a fling of his head, tossing his hair into the air as he slid the coat on. A moment later he was past Andy, footfalls echoing from the restroom.

Andy focused on the man now standing in the bus doorway. He too, wore a drover, only darker and made of leather. He stood on the bottom step, smoking a cigarette.

Andy started for the bus.

The man in the doorway saw the stranger approaching and pinched the cigarette out between his fingers and stuffed the remainder into a coat pocket.

As Andy neared, he could see inside the bus through the windows. Another man was lying in a hammock hanging from the roof. That was five, maybe there wouldn't be room for him. Closer, Andy could hear voices from the far side of the bus as the young man in the doorway continued to watch him.

"You ready?" the voice was young, alto.

"Let 'er rip," the other voice, also young but lower, replied. An electric motor started, a gurgling noise soon following.

"Whoa! This shit stinks," the alto said.

"Wha'd'ya expect? It is shit."

Then Andy was at the bus, a whiff of the tobacco still in the vicinity. Andy knew the smell. It had been some years, but he recognized the aroma of euphoria.

"Evening," the man in the doorway said.

"Good evening," Andy greeted, extending his hand. "Name's Bucansin. Andy Bucansin."

The man in the leather drover stepped off the bus and shook Andy's hand. "Z. Can I help you?" He had seen Andy emerge from the building as they pulled in, watched him watch for a while, then walk across the empty parking lot straight to them. He knew what Andy wanted.

"I was wondering if I could catch a lift to Laramie?" Andy asked, knowing they had to be going at least that far.

Z looked Andy over from head to toe and back up again. "I have no problem with it. We'll have to check with the rest of the band, though."

A wet, sucking sound came from the other side of the bus, then the electric motor went silent. Then, "Whew! That there has to be Z. He's so full of himself," the second voice bellowed.

"Reed, he didn't leave the bus," the first voice hushed.

There was a pause, a muffled giggle, then "Oops."

Z smiled at Andy, "They love me, really."

"Ah, shit!" Reed complained. "I got that crap on my hands. Ewwwww."

Ponytail came around the bus, hands held out from his sides, headed across the parking lot. Andy and Z turned their heads to him and watched as he walked away.

A moment after Ponytail disappeared around the building, the man with the dreadlocks came around the corner.

"That was Reed, he's our wind man," Z said as he and Andy watched dreadlocks approach. "That there heading for us is Kip. He plays bass. Finishing up on the other side is Thorton. He's our lead singer and drummer." Z pointed a thumb behind him into the bus, "Jointer's crashed in the hammock: back-up vocals, lead and rhythm guitar."

"And you?" Andy queried.

"Keyboard."

"Who's your friend?" Kip asked Z, stopping beside Z.

"He's looking for a lift to Laramie."

"You going to Laramie?" Kip asked the stranger.

"Actually," Andy said, "I'm headed for Nevada. A few miles outside of Las Vegas. A town called Indian Springs."

"Well, hell," Kip said, holding his arms wide, "We're going to L.A. We can drop you off at 'Vegas."

Z turned to Kip and shot him a glance that Andy missed.

Kip looked Andy over, from head to toe and back up. "Hell, he smokes."

Andy knew he meant - the whiff as he arrived at the bus. "If you mean what I smelled when I walked up here, I haven't smoked weed in years," he whispered. "But I won't say anything, if that's what you're concerned about."

Thorton came from behind the bus and joined the trio. "Who's this?" he questioned his friends.

"Guy bumming a ride from us. Looks like he could use a joint, too," Kip summed up, then turned to Andy. "What's your name, dude?"

Andy put out his hand to Kip, "Andy Bucansin. Nice to meet you, Kip."

Kip gawked at Andy, then realized the obvious. "Z introduce everyone?"

Andy nodded. "I sure appreciate the ride." He turned to Z, "I'll buy the next round of gas, to show my thanks."

Z nodded. "Sounds like a deal."

Andy turned to Thorton, hand out. "Thorton, right?"

Thorton nodded.

"Aren't you cold?" Andy asked.

Thorton shook Andy's hand. "A little," then stepped into the bus, stopping halfway up the stairs. He turned around and called to Andy. "Climb aboard," he said with a wave of his hand. "There ain't much room, but it's warm." He climbed up the remaining few stairs and walked towards the back of the bus.

"Kip will show you where you can put your bag," Z said, motioning to Kip with his head.

"Come on, dude. You'll like this," Kip said before he boarded the bus.

Andy followed Kip into the bus, the warmth inside tingling his skin.

"You can thank Z for the bus. It's a 'fifty-nine Chevy Superior. Only has twenty-six thousand miles on it."

"What year is it?" Andy queried.

"Nineteen fifty-nine. Z says he found it in some small town's impound lot. It was retired during it's first year of service because some kid had a seizure on it and died on the way to school one morning. The boys mother went hysterical and almost killed herself. She said the bus was possessed.

"So, they stuffed it away; way in the back of the impound yard. Where it sat for forty-one years until Z found it. Z designed the layout and did most all the work himself," Kip explained as he stuffed Andy's backpack under the seat behind the driver. It was the only original seat left in the bus. "With our help."

"Helped a lot," Thorton boasted from the dining table near the rear of the bus, driver's side.

Z stepped into the bus, stopping at the top of the steps. He leaned against the driver's seat as he waited for the path to clear. "Why don't you take that seat by the stove in the back?" he suggested to Andy, pointing to a single, plush, recliner-like chair near the back, on the right side of the bus. It sat between a copper-clad, marine, wood-burning stove in the corner and the 'kitchen' that ran from the front to about midway down; a small refrigerator, sink and counter, and a two-burner gas stove and oven. The chair sat askew, so when the footrest was out it blocked the aisle.

Andy sidestepped the sleeping Jointer in the hammock and sat in the cloth seat, sinking into the cushion as the heat from the lit stove flushed his face. He unlaced his boots and slid them off, unbuttoned the outer layers of shirts, then leaned against the back of the chair and looked across the aisle out the window.

Kip stood beside Jointer hanging in the hammock. He grabbed one side of the hammock and rocked it, jerking Jointer awake. "Time to get up, Stoner," he said to the groggy Jointer.

"We in L.A.?" Jointer asked, then stretched.

"Not hardly. It's your turn to drive."

Ten minutes later, after a trip to the restroom, Jointer started the bus and pulled onto the interstate. Andy was already asleep.

Chapter III

The bus jerked into the next lane, swinging Andy awake in the hammock. Andy turned and twisted until he could see the driver, expecting to see Jointer. He gasped when he saw the golden spider from the last dream at the wheel.

In the mirror above the driver, Arabella turned one of six eyes to Andy. "Thanks for the ride," she said, her voice like warm honey.

Andy blinked. Ride? She was driving, and poorly, too. "No, thank you, Arabella." He couldn't believe his poise. Nor his words. "Where are we going?" Andy asked as he rolled out of the hammock and onto his feet. Hadn't he fallen asleep in a chair?

He looked around the bus, holding on to the hammock for balance as Arabella continued to swerve the bus back and forth. The kitchen, the plush chair, everything was gone except the hammock and the seat behind the driver. And there was something new. Hanging in a web stretched across the back of the bus was Z, the only other person on the bus. Andy moved towards Z, Arabella watching in the mirror.

Z's eyes were closed. "Z? You okay? Z?" *Andy reached out and touched him on the chest.* "Z?!"

Z's eyes snapped open, glaring at Andy. "I was asleep," *he barked.*

Andy, startled, stepped back once, then back up to Z. "Is she okay to drive?"

Z peeked over Andy and met one of Arabella's six eyes in the mirror. "I don't know. She's your spider. Ask to see her license. Now leave me alone. I'm driving next." *Z closed his eyes and dropped his head.*

Andy turned towards the front. He saw Arabella looking at him in the mirror before she diverted her eyes. Cautiously, but without fear, he moved forward.

"Everything's going to be fine," *Arabella said when Andy sat in the seat behind her, her voice appearing in his mind, sensual, familiar.*

"Where is everyone?" *Andy asked Arabella.*

"Asleep."

Andy looked around. There were only the three of them. "Where are we going?" *he asked.*

Arabella glanced an eye to the mirror, the swerving of the bus perpetual, a faded blue pendulum veering down the freeway. She rotated her head, turning her fangs to him and leaning close, "Everything's going to be fine."

Andy pushed himself back into the seat. It was difficult enough for him to fathom talking to Arabella at all and now, with her fangs inches from his face she says everything is going to be fine. He was glad Z was there, but wished he wasn't tied up.

"Shouldn't you be watching the road?" *he said to the fangs, trying to get her to turn away from him.*

"I'm watching over you," *she told him in a whisper.*

Andy could feel her breath that time. It was hot, moist, and smelled of brownies.

"Brownies?" Andy muttered.

Andy's amazement made Arabella laugh. A soft, cotton giggle. She rotated back to the front. "Jointer makes them," she said, an eye in the mirror on Andy. "They are heaven."

Andy just sat, trying to remember what happened before he went to sleep. His mind filled with images of webs and spiders and silent missiles. He squished his eyes and shook his head, but the images remained.

"Everything's going to be fine," Arabella repeated.

There was a confidence in her voice that calmed him, but still he felt uneasy, surreal. Her voice vibrated the images Andy saw, blurring them. Slowly they came back into focus, only now they were Dali-like memories of his grandparents farm; milking the cows, pitching hay, pitching woo with the neighbors niece.

Then Andy saw his parents laughing, sitting next to a wall a few tables away in a restaurant. Suddenly, the water heater on the other side of the wall exploded and Andy's mother was thrown into the table next to him, her clothing on fire. She fell to the floor, limp.

Andy looked from his mother, motionless on the floor, to his father standing, framed by the hole in the wall; his head, left arm and shoulder missing. He hovered several seconds before crumbling to the floor.

Andy began to tremble. He could feel the tears and grief crawl through his soul and time towards his voice. Tears flowed down his cheeks as the internal trembling became more violent. He did not want to cry. Not over his parents, not again. But now he knew; knew what happened to his father, knew what his mother saw and grandfather knew.

A convulsion ripped through Andy and the image flipped like a channel change to his mother lying in the hospital. Tubes were in her nose, mouth and arms. She was wrapped in bandages that were yellow stained and moist, her face flat. Her one exposed eye held an expression of sadness that touched Andy, even now.

The wailing was close, he could feel it pushing through his grip.

"You have to let it out, Andrew. Let it out and put them behind you. You have to move on."

Andy looked up into the mirror at Arabella. Arabella looked back with four of her six eyes.

Lips trembling and voice breaking, Andy said, "Why did you show me that? Why?"

"You wanted to know."

And he had. For years he had wanted to know. Now he wished he could take it back.

Arabella slammed on the brakes, putting the bus into a nosedive and lurching Andy into the railing in front of him. When the bus stopped Arabella reached a leg over to the lever and opened the door.

"This is your stop," *she said, all eyes in the mirror.*

Andy stared at Arabella a moment. Off? What about Z?

Arabella looked from the mirror to Andy, as if she knew what he was thinking. "Everything is going to be fine," *she said.* "He drives next."

Andy suddenly felt at ease. He turned and stepped off the bus into the middle of a cobweb that stretched to the horizons. Veils of dense, grey cobweb hung like drapery around him. There was no sound, no breeze, no hot or cold. Suddenly he felt alone, and empty. He spun around to climb back on the bus but it wasn't there, only cobweb curtains.

"Hello?" *he called out, his voice timid, unsure. Who was he calling to, anyway?*

"Everything's going to be fine", *came a sweet, feminine voice that belonged to a child. Out of the cobweb grey a small girl walked into focus. She wore a yellow dress that billowed to the knees, black lace trimming the hem. Her hands were clasped to her belly, gently holding something. Her hair was golden and aglow, as if lit by sunlight; but there was no sun. She looked up at Andy, then held out her hands, exposing a large Orb spider, similar to*

Frequency Seven

Arabella, sitting in her palms. "You just have to trust her."

"Arabella?" Andy asked quietly, still on the verge of tears.

"Yes," the little girl responded.

Her green eyes gazed into Andy's with a warmth that caused him to shudder. He wanted to cry, but couldn't. Not in front of this little girl. Andy sniffed, then asked,

"Can you go now? I've something I have to..to take care of."

"That is why I am here; to help."

"Help with what?" Andy sniffed frequently now, tears streaming freely down his cheeks. "I don't know you."

"I am Tabitha." She raised her arms to him. "I am a part of you, silly."

Andy laughed as images of Yin-Yang flashed through his mind. Was she a part of him? Just what the hell was going on? He fell to his knees, bright flecks of web dust puffing into the still air. He looked through watery eyes at the little girl in yellow. Her image was wavy, fuzzy, and held a pull of security he reached for. He raised his arms to her, outstretched, beckoning her to him.

Tabitha floated more than she walked to Andy. She dropped the spider and it dispersed into the air before landing. She held her arms out to Andy. When she reached him, he pulled her close, tight.

They melted together, the front of Tabitha blending with the front of Andy. Her head sunk into his chest, their arms folding into the other. Andy began to bawl; grief and sorrow for his parents that had been buried for years coming out in wails that vibrated the surrounding web.

The spider Tabitha had dropped moments before now reappeared, hovering in front of Andy's open mouth as if dangling from a dragline. It was almost touching Andy's lips. Then Andy gasped for breath, gulping in air and the spider. He didn't notice the spider and continued to sob, emotion jerking his frame. He swallowed.

Tabitha stroked the back of Andy's head, soothing him with cooing sounds and reassuring whispers of, "Everything's going to be fine".

Andy awoke to a motionless bus, echoes of Tabitha's voice in his ears. He was slouched in the chair, nearly prone with his feet in the aisle. He turned his head. The band was gone. Then Andy felt something move on his chest. He looked down his body.

In the middle of his chest, one leg propped on a button, all six eyes staring at him, was the yellow spider. *"Morning, Andrew."* Her voice was suddenly in his head. It was honey-like.

"Arabella," Andy acknowledged quietly with a slight nod. He felt relaxed, well slept. This last dream had been a release of ancient emotions.

Arabella raised the leg off the button, *"You trust me, then?"* She rested her leg back on the button.

"Yes, I do." The confidence in his own voice surprised him. Was this really happening? He felt awake, but yet he had to still be dreaming.

Arabella touched her fangs to his shirt, dipping the front of her body as if bowing. *"Everythi..."*

"I know, everything's going to be fine," Andy finished for her. Again, he sounded confident. He was losing it. He was sure of it now.

Arabella bowed again, then dropped off Andy and scurried to his backpack under the front seat.

Andy blinked then rolled out of the chair. He knew he was awake when his head spun and neck kinked. He looked at his backpack. "I'll be damned," he muttered, then bent at the waist and looked out the window. "I wonder where we are?"

As he put his boots on, Andy continued to look out the windows. It was still dark. They were at a truck stop, parked along side the pumps. Laramie. Kip was manning the refueling process, dancing a jig in an effort to keep warm.

Andy thought about his grandmother as he laced up his boots. She would believe him if he told her about Arabella and the dreams. Grandma was New Age before New Age even had a name. He had thought her scary when he first went to live there after his parents' deaths. But over the years he had grown to love her as much as he did his mother.

Grandma was the one that taught him about nature. She showed him the wonder and awe of sunrise and sunset, and the power of the stars. She often spoke of Indian lore when she described Nature, using their examples to get a point across. She introduced him to gardening, vegetables and herbs. She helped him in understanding all creatures, including spiders. She had said spiders brought good luck. Said they were natures bug spray. A spider in the kitchen prevents a summer of itchin'. She always liked rhymes.

The rapport with nature he acquired on grandparent's farm he thought everyone had until he was in his mid teens. But this was a first - conversing with an arachnid. Andy shook his head and left the bus, pausing by his bag, tempted to look inside, but didn't. He wasn't sure of what was happening, and the truth right now may just upset things. He needed to talk to Grandma.

When Andy came out of the truck stop restroom, he called his grandmother in Illinois from a payphone in the hallway, collect.

"What do you mean I can't talk to Granma, Old Man? Why can't you tell me where she is?"

"She asked me not to let you know."

"Know what?"

"She made me promise."

"Grandpa..come on. You gotta tell me what's going on with Granma." Silence from the other end. "I'll call Wilma and find out what's up," Andy threatened. Wilma was a family friend and town gossip.

"All right, Boy. Don't get your britches all twisted." A pause. A moment of telephone static. "Your grandmother's in the hospital."

"Grandma's where?" He had just seen them six months ago. They were both healthy as ever. "I'll be home as soon as I can get a plane ticket."

"No need for that, Boy. She's only gettin' them silicone things put in. The doctor thought at her age she should stay.."

"She's having *what* put in?"

"Them silicone in-plants; to make her look bigger."

"She's what!?? She's sixty-seven for heaven's sake. Who she trying to impress? You?"

"Watch your mouth." Another moment of static. "You know how she is. Besides, she'll be a lot more funner to hug when you visit."

Andy dropped the receiver he laughed so hard. When he regained control of himself several moments later, he picked up the dangling handset.

"Andrew? You there, boy?"

"I'm here, Old Man. I dropped the phone."

"You dropped it 'cause you was laughing. What were you laughing at?"

"Somebody walked by, Old Man. I think he's from California. Anything about my truck?" There was silence on the line. "Gramps?"

"They found your truck." His tone was solemn.

"What's wrong with it? Are the tools gone?"

"They pulled it out of the Platte the other day."

"He dumped it in the river?!?" Andy glanced up and down the hall to see if anyone heard his outburst. The hallway was empty.

"I checked with your insurance today. They said they'd send a check in a couple days."

"Couple days. Yeah, right." He paused for a moment. "I'll call you when I get to Moses' and see how Grandma's doing, and if the check came."

"How long will that be?"

"I dunno. Few days at the most. Depends on how many stops my ride makes."

"Why don't you just buy a bus ticket to get there?"

"Now come on, we've gone through this before. Besides, I am taking a bus."

"Let me send you some then, when you get to Moses'."

"We've been through that before, too. Besides, Moses will take care of me."

"Yeah, I know he will. I still don't understand your silly ass. But Mother says to let you do things your way."

"I love you, Grandpa."

"I love you too, Son. You take care, now."

"Talk to you in a few days." Andy laughed again as he hung up the phone, picturing his little grandmother Partonized; then wondered just how big she did get them. He would have to wait to tell her about Arabella and his dreams, Grandpa just wouldn't understand. He pondered the meanings of the dreams and how Grandma was going to look as he wandered around the truck stop searching for members of the band. He found Z down the aisle with magazines and medicine. He was reading a comic book, science fiction.

"Ever read Lovecraft?" Andy asked, fixated on the cover of the magazine Z held.

"Everything he's written." Z looked at Andy out of the corner of his eye. "Want my list of favorite authors?" he threatened.

Andy raised his hands defensively, "Just asking", then glanced to the floor. Z returned to the comic book, Andy turned his gaze to its cover where a scantily dressed woman was being eaten by a spider. A spider that resembled Arabella. Andy shuddered.

Z caught Andy's movement in his peripheral vision and looked at Andy. "I'm going to buy it. You can read it after I'm done."

"Hunh? No. I..I was just looking at the picture."

Z flipped over the comic book and looked at the cover, upside-down. As he returned the book to its original position, he said, "Cute. Shame she's being eaten."

"Actually, I was looking at the spider."

The comic book flipped again, then Z righted it by crossing his arms. "It's a Golden Orb; nephila clavipes. Common in Florida."

"How the hell do you know that?" Andy's tone blatantly calling Z a liar.

Z closed the magazine and dropped his arms to his sides. "I made it up," he said indignantly. Z headed up the aisle towards the cashier.

Andy stood there, knowing he had said the wrong thing, wondering if he should start looking for another ride, when Z stopped and turned around.

"You coming?"

Andy nodded, then caught up to Z.

"Us long hairs got to stick together," Z said when Andy reached him.

"Thanks," Andy said. "Thought maybe I lost my ride just then."

"Phfft. Not for something that petty. Besides, your getting the gas tab. Right?"

"Right."

As they walked out the door to the tarmac, Andy asked Z, "You made up a name like nephilia clappers?"

Z smiled at Andy's mispronunciation. He almost corrected Andy, then thought against it.

Chapter IV

As Glass Reality and a guest rolled across Wyoming through the wee hours, Arabella spun a web under the front seat. Andy sat at the dining table, facing the back of the bus, Z across the table facing him. Jointer was at the wheel, focused on driving. Thorton sat behind Jointer, accentuating the pulse of the bus by drumming on the handrail. Kip laid in the hammock strung overhead, just behind Thorton, swinging in rhythm with the bus, asleep. Reed, softly adding a flute melody to Thorton's beat, sat in the chair Andy had slept in. Z was reading his latest comic book acquisition - *TIME WARP*, the one with the picture of the woman being devoured by a spider on the cover.

"How come you know so much about spiders?" Andy suddenly threw at Z.

Z lowered the comic book and gave Andy a look of annoyance. "I read a lot."

"Obviously more than just comic books."

Z laid the magazine on the table, put his elbows on the book and leaned closer to Andy. "I've got a Bachelor's in Entomology." Z brushed a tuft of hair away from his face and pointed across the bus. "Reed has a Bachelor's in music, working on his Master's. He writes most of our music. Thorton is studying astronomy, and Kip and Jointer each have a Bachelor's in Computer Science. We're not airheads. We just don't like the 9-to-5 routine."

"Neither do I."

"What *do* you do?" Z quizzed Andy.

"Up until last week I was a wandering contractor."

"What the hell is that?" Reed blurted.

"I go from town to town doing odd jobs for people. I'd look in the local paper for the jobs. I'd do anything from building porches and running fences to fixing cars and making air boats."

"Versatile sum'bitch, ain't ya'," Reed observed.

"Ok, so what happened last week?"

"My truck and tools were stolen by the last guy I worked for; back in Omaha."

"That's a bitch. Have they found him, yet?"

"No. But they did find my truck. At the bottom of a river."

"He drove it into a river?"

"Why not? I helped him make an airboat."

"The ones with the big propeller on the back?"

Andy nodded. "Apparently he used my truck to tow the boat to the river, launched the boat, then drowned my truck."

"That's a real bitch. Were you insured?"

"Yeah, but who knows how long it'll take to get a check. My grandfather talked to the insurance company and they told him they'll mail the check in a few days."

"So, it'll be waiting for you when you get home?"

Andy shook his head. "I don't live in Indian Springs. An old friend lives close by. The insurance check will go to my grandparents, back in Illinois. They'll mail it to me at Moses'."

"Your friend in Indian Springs?"

"Yeah. I haven't seen him in a while and thought I'd spend the winter there. You know, winter in the desert. He offered after hearing about my truck." Andy then shrugged before adding, "He's like a brother to me."

"Sounds like a plan."

Andy nodded, still curious about the spider and what else Z might know. "What college did you attend?"

"We all went to the University of Minnesota, at Duluth." Z halfheartedly pushed a fist into the air. "Go Bulldogs."

"What else can you tell me about the spider on your comic book?"

Reed went back to playing his flute. He knew all about Z and did not care about bugs.

"Not much. Entomology is the study of insects, not arachnids. But I did study spiders a bit, and ..." Z leaned back and looked up, recalling his studies. "The species on the cover has the strongest natural fiber in its dragline silk." He looked back at Andy. "Tropical ones have been known to make webs eighteen feet across. They catch birds in those big webs. Umm-mm, that's all I can remember."

"This is gonna sound crazy."

"We've heard crazy before."

"Like spiders that talk."

The flute stopped. "That's a rather odd," Reed interjected. Thorton, oblivious to the conversation behind him, tapped on. There was a moment of charged silence. Then Z spoke.

"Go on."

"In my dreams. Or just coming out of them. She doesn't really talk a whole lot. It's more pictures. Metaphors."

Z put his hands on the sides of his face and propped his elbows on the table. "She? Do tell."

Andy inhaled deeply, ran a hand through his hair, then said, "I've been having these dreams. Vivid, realistic dreams."

Reed and Z exchanged several glances as Andy told them about the spider controlled puppet and the silent missile launch. They exchanged several more when he told them about Arabella driving the bus with Z webbed in the back.

He had told them all he could remember about his dreams. But not everything. He did not tell them about Tabitha. It was time for their opinion about these obscure nightmares. "Well."

"Well, what?" Reed returned.

"Can a spider influence dreams?" Andy asked, looking at Z.

Z scooted out from behind the table and stood in the aisle. "They're suppose to bring good luck or something, but I've never heard of them with any psychic ability," he said, then plopped both hands on the table and peered out the window. The sun was brightening the horizon, long shadows clinging to the ground; Z could almost see them shorten. He stood straight and turned towards the front of the bus.

"Jointer?" he called. "Suns coming up."

"Duh," came the reply from the front.

"Pull over first chance you get."

"Duh."

"Geez," Z said under his breath.

"Start rolling," Jointer said as the bus slowed to searching speed.

"Where are the skins?"

Skins. Rolling papers. Andy looked to the floor. It had been years since he last smoked weed. He can remember why he quit, too. It's illegal. While Thorton and Z broke up the weed, Andy could not come up with any other reason on why not to smoke marijuana. As they started to roll joints, he silently hoped one would be rolled for him. It had been too long.

*   *   *

Frequency Seven

Twenty minutes passed before Jointer found a suitable spot. A mile down a dirt road he parked the bus near an outcropping of rocks. In the back of the bus, Reed, Thorton, Z and Andy sat around the table, five joints lined up in the center of the tray. Kip sat in the hammock, sorting dreadlocks to either side of his head when Jointer strolled to the back of the bus.

"He's got 'em numbered," Jointer said upon reaching the table, pointing a thumb at Kip.

"Shut up, Stoner," came Kip's sharp retort.

Andy looked up at Jointer. Jointer, who was staring at the five joints, had shoulder length hair. "Why stoner?"

"If he could," Kip explained, "he'd stay stoned all the time."

"Five? Who's driving?" Jointer queried.

"That's yet to be decided," Z said.

"Well, let's go," Jointer said as he reached towards the tray.

Reed slapped Jointer's hand away. "I'll take them out. You lead the way."

"Give me one to light on the way out," Jointer demanded.

"It's ten feet. Go," Reed ordered as he stood. "You're blocking the way."

"Asshole," Jointer whined. "Some of that is mine, you know."

"I know," Reed said. "You can have one all to yourself. Just like everyone else. But not until you're outside." He waved at Jointer, shooing him on. "Now, would you mind?"

Jointer stomped to the front of the bus and leaped outside.

"What a bunch of babies," Z said to no one in particular.

Reed picked up three joints and stood, handing one of the joints to Kip. "I'll drive," Thorton volunteered.

Z nodded. "I'll tell Joint-Man outside," he said, then nudged Andy in the ribs. "Pick one of them doobies and slide out."

Kip and Reed were headed for the door as Andy twisted his legs into the aisle behind them. Andy then grabbed one of the two remaining joints off the tray, stood and walked to the door.

Outside the bus, standing by a group of large rocks, Glass Reality and a guest watched as dawn awoke the land. The ground sloped down to another hill half a mile away. Trees skirted rocks and tall grass encroached on every opening.

Clouds, dark in front of the sun, trimmed with golden fire, shielded Andy's eyes as he peered east. Trees, near and far, were topped in painted sunlight, the shadow left by the night still clawing at the ground.

Andy exhaled and suddenly felt a closeness to nature he had not felt even back on Grandpa's dairy farm. Here, now, all life around him, from his fellow humans to the microbes in the soil, seemed connected to him on a subatomic level. Electron to electron type of thing. He shuddered. A moment later, when the sun peeked through a cloud, Andy could feel its full spectrum on his face and hands; the cosmic pattern warming the skin.

Yet, as the sun pulled itself from the clouds and his companions oohed and awed, Andy felt the visitor. Even through the subatomic intimacy of the moment, he still felt an alien on his own planet, an outsider everywhere, alone even in crowds. Alone, even now.

Suddenly, Arabella was in his mind. And just as suddenly, he didn't feel that alone anymore. Andy chased away the remaining alienation with another hit from the joint, pushing the essence of the isolation from his mind by watching the distant hills awaken with sunlit dew.

On the fringes of his hearing he heard footfalls, gravel crunching and remote voices of other humans. He exhaled smoke into the sun's rays, losing the feeling of the stranger in the ballooning purple haze hovering in front of him.

"Enjoying the morning?" Z said.

Andy floated out of the purple balloon and stepped up to his eyes. "Quite nice," Andy lulled out. "The sun feels exquisite."

"Exquisite?" Z leaned towards Andy, peering into his eyes. "You're stoned."

"Uh, duh."

"Duh," echoed Z. Andy began to giggle. Z shook his head, smiling. "Come on. The others are on the bus waiting."

"I'll just be another minute. This is beautiful."

Z turned and watched the sunrise with Andy. After a moment Z said, "This is what life's about, being able to watch a gorgeous sunrise, stoned."

*   *   *

Thorton eased the bus onto the pavement as Andy climbed into the hammock and laid down, head to the rear of the bus. Z sat on the right side of the bus watching the scenery go by. Reed and Kip sat at the table reading comic books, Jointer in the forward seat playing his guitar through headphones. Andy then noticed the web and Arabella under the front seat.

Andy lit the remainder of his joint while watching Arabella knit under the front seat. She was putting the final wraps around something she had caught while they were enjoying the sunrise. She looked bigger. Andy had a quick flash of empathy for Arabella's meal, but knew this was the way it had to be, always was, and always will. Minutes later, the joint out and laying in a small, stone ashtray on the kitchen counter, he drifted off to sleep.

Andy watched, amazed, compelled to witness Arabella feed; as if it would help in his understanding of her. Even from across the bus Andy could see Arabella sink her fangs into the silken ball, injecting her fluid.

Andy had begun to wonder how he could view the act, when he realized he was in her realm again. He tensed, the hammock straightening, the focus on Arabella distorting, causing the image to run. Two eyes moved off her victim and onto Andy.

"Shh." The whisper slid through his head. Andy relaxed, the hammock

slacking to an arc.

Suddenly he was no longer in the hammock. Arabella, the web, and the bus were gone.

Andy was standing inside a stone room, a cave. Overhead a hole let in a shaft of sunlight, illuminating the room in a hazy, natural glow. Andy turned slowly in a circle examining the room. There was no door, the only opening the hole in the ceiling. The floor was fine dirt. On the walls were crude paintings in red, yellow and black, depictions of people, buffalo, coyote, and spiders. A yellow spider was on the wall directly across from him.

A hide drum began to play, heavy on the first of seven beats. Andy scanned the chamber again. There was no one else in the room. There was no drum. Not even a painting of one. Then the painted yellow spider on the wall began to move, stepping to the beat.

When the painted spider had moved halfway around the room, the beat began to slow. The volume then increased, resonating through the rock. The spider stopped walking and began to vibrate in sympathy to the rhythm.

Andy began to feel strange. His entire body felt as though it was being squeezed. It was difficult to breath. A pressure was building on his ears and eyes, pushing inward. Nausea suddenly overtook him and he swooned. On the way to the ground, his view blurry and fading, Andy saw the walls undulating.

As he lay face up on the ground, the air itself seeming to constrict around him, Andy felt the ground rolling beneath him in waves. In the tunneling blackness, Andy saw the spider leap from the wall and land inches from his face, then all went dark.

Andy lay still, eyes shut, as he demanded response from his body, waiting helplessly for the painted spider to devour him. He wanted to get up and run, but he ached, his muscles and insides felt like sponge.

He opened his eyes with caution; it felt like cotton was being pressed firmly against them. Above him was a blurry sky, the colors of the rainbow quilted across the unfocused blue background of the image. He now laid across a large web. The stone room was gone. He closed his eyes again.

He tried to move his arm to wipe his face but found the arm wouldn't move. He didn't feel tied or strapped down, just that his body didn't work anymore. Then a vibration shot his eyes open.

This vibration was different. It was more of a shaking, a trembling, like someone walking on a tight rope. Or a web.

"Arabella?" Andy queried the fuzz, his vision still unfocused. He hoped it was her, unable to even turn his head to look around.

"Yes," came the soothing reply into his mind.

"I'm..stuck."

"The web does not hold you, Andrew."

Andy tried to move again, struggling against himself. "Then..what?" Andy thought more than spoke. "Am I paralyzed?" he asked aloud.

"No," came the response.

"Then..."

"Your body has heard the whispers of Hell. It needs time to heal," Arabella placed in his head. "Remember that beat."

"The beat?" Andy barely recalled what happened. "What was the beat, Arabella? I..I don't remember much before now."

Silence. There had been no vibrations, she was still here. Andy's vision was still blurry as he finally turned his head, but all he could distinguish was different colors and some sense of depth. On his left, where he thought Arabella was, was a distant, jagged horizon of dark brown. Past his feet lay only the blurry, patchwork of blue sky. On his right was a little girl, vivid and clear against the blurry background.

"Tabitha?!" he said, startled.

"Do you not remember me?"

There was a pause as Andy tried to comprehend her visual clarity amidst the surrounding blur. "Yes, I remember you."

"Then why do you question?"

"Guess I'm not too sure about anything right now."
"You do know where you are, do you not?"
Andy slowly shook his head, "No."
"I cannot exist without you, Andrew. Does that give you an idea?"

Andy closed his eyes. He had gone mad, he thought. Inside his own mind and he had no control. He tried to move again; to raise an arm, wiggle a finger, something besides just his head. There. His left leg. His foot moved. He moved it again. Yes. He bent the knee and his foot fell through the webbing, a cross strand catching his leg just above the knee. He did the same with his right leg, then slowly, clumsily, pulled himself up to a sitting position, holding on to the strands white knuckled as he sat on a strand as if on a tree branch.

He opened his eyes after his head stopped spinning, then looked to his right. Tabitha was still the only thing in focus, she was smiling. *"Told you I was here to help. Jump down. I have something to show you."* She waved her hand, gesturing for him to follow as she turned and started walking away, the strands of the web parting before her, rejoining after she had passed.

Andy checked his grip on the strands and gazed to the fuzzy green below. It looked close. He slid off the web, hoping the green was grass. He hovered for a moment, waist even with the web, then slowly descended as if in an elevator to the thick grass below. It was then, as his feet touched the green, that his vision came to focus, the web rising over his head several feet before stopping. It hovered there, as if it had a purpose.

They were in a flat, grassy field that reached to the horizon. The grass was short, thick, and cool, giving his bare feet a natural carpet. Andy looked to the sky through the web. In the blue that filled the overhead, amoebae patches in the red spectrum grew and faded, characteristic of a mood ring. He watched as if watching a fire burn, staring mesmerized for moments that lasted hours before he heard Tabitha call to him, *"Come, Andrew. We will be there soon."*

When Andy caught up with Tabitha the landscape changed. Suddenly they were approaching a lone cement pillar in a desert flat, the coarse sand hot under his feet. The air, also heated, dried his mouth and nose. The pillar, five feet in height and three in diameter, was the only thing above ground within sight. As they neared, details focused in: at the top of the pillar were square holes, two horizontal rows of four holes, each hole facing a different angle as if it were a concert speaker. The rest of the pillar was seamless, unmarred. The sky overhead was a patchless blue.

"We need to be behind it," Tabitha said when she reached the pillar, continuing on around.

Andy stopped at the front, peering into the horns. "What's it for?"

"It unleashes Hell, Andrew. A silent Hell. Quickly, before it comes on."

Andy leaped to Tabitha's side behind the pillar. "Shouldn't we back a way a bit further, then?" The pillar was solid on this side. They faced the expanse they had just left, and a city skyline on the horizon.

Andy guestimated they were between five and ten miles from the city. Then, without warning, without any flash of light, explosion or sound, the buildings simply crumbled before his eyes. Movement in his peripheral vision caused him to look up.

The sky, although still blue, was rippling like a pond after a stone's throw. The web remained motionless as the ripples, trimmed in crimson, fanned out towards the fallen city from the pillar in front of them. Andy looked to Tabitha.

"What happened?"

"Hell, Andrew. Deadly, silent Hell." The sound of the city falling reached them then, muffled by the distance. "The same thing that happened to you at the Indian cave," Tabitha continued. "Only then it was not so intense. Or focused."

"How do you know all this? If you're suppose to be me, that is."

"Arabella."

"Arabella?"

Tabitha stared up at Andy, amazed. "We do get denser as we get *older."*

"That's not funny. Or nice."

"How do you think Arabella talks to you, silly?"

Andy shrugged.

"Tsk. Through me," Tabitha tipped her head to one side as though impatient.

Andy looked back at the rubble on the horizon. "She wasn't..over there, was she?"

"Arabella?"

Andy nodded.

"No," she giggled.

Andy, still gazing at the crumpled city, asked, "The buildings were empty, weren't they?"

"No."

Andy, again, awoke to a motionless bus. He laid in the hammock looking out the window, wondering what was going on in his dreams, what they meant. They were at another truck stop, Thorton with the refueling duties this time. Again, the rest of the band was gone.

Andy rolled off the hammock and walked to the front of the bus. Stepping off he turned back to view under the seat behind the driver. Arabella was near the center of her web, as if watching him leave.

Once on the tarmac, Andy noticed that it was noon. He had slept through the morning. He put his forearm across his belly as he headed for the building. He was hungry. Quite, in fact. Andy wondered briefly if they were staying long enough for him to go to the restaurant. A steak, mashed potatoes and gravy, dressing, and a side of green beans on a warm plate menued in his mind's eye. But, a tuna sandwich and some fruit would be just as good. A sign in the window informed him that he was in Rock Springs, Wyoming; elevation 6271 feet. Andy opened the door. Maybe Z would know about the device in his dream.

Frequency Seven

Inside, Andy kept an eye out for Z as he searched the store for edibles. After finding a sandwich and an apple, Andy stood by the yogurt machine, filling a large cup with the chocolate flavor.

"Man, we thought you were going to crash all the way to 'Vegas," Kip said from behind.

Andy put a spoon in the cup and turned to Kip. "I didn't know I was going to sleep at all. Seen Z?"

"Should be back on the bus. We'll be ready to go after I pay for gas."

They started for the register, Kip leading the way through the narrow aisles eating his apple.

"Kip? Can I ask ya' something?"

*   *   *

Andy stepped over Reed stocking the shelves of the bus' kitchen, making his way to the rear and Z, who sat at the table. Thorton sat in the recliner, drumsticks tapping lightly on his thigh. Jointer sat behind the driver, reading one of Z's comic books. As Andy sat down at the table, Kip closed the door and started the bus.

"'Vegas is our next stop. Where you want us to drop you off?" Z said from the table.

"I've got an address in my bag. I'll get it when I'm done," Andy said, raising the sandwich.

"No rush. It's about a ten hour ride to 'Vegas."

The bus rocked and bumped as they left the truck stop. Andy watched out the window, eating his small meal, his mind filled with the latest dream. Only now the dream seemed like a memory, like he had actually been there. Reed finished stocking the supplies and joined them at the table. When Kip shifted into the last gear, Andy turned to Z.

"You know a device that can level a city without any explosion, light or noise of any kind? And I mean the whole city."

Kip looked at the trio in the mirror over the windshield. He wish he could hear what they were saying. He, too, was curious about this leveling of a city, but when Andy had asked him about, all he could do was shrug.

"Where'd you come up with that?" Z said.

"You wouldn't believe me if I told you." Andy spooned chocolate yogurt into his mouth.

Z looked at him with suspicion. "That spider?"

"Another dream."

"Sounds more like a nightmare," Reed said.

"Hmph." Andy swallowed. "I suppose it was."

"So, what happened in your dream?" Reed probed.

Andy finished his yogurt as he described his dream to Reed and Z. Reed listened acutely, leaning on the table towards Andy. Z sat as if he had heard it before.

When Andy had finished, Z thought a moment, then said, "I'd say the ripples in the sky were caused by the device. Maybe symbolic of what was going on."

"Maybe, but that does little good," Andy leaned into the aisle and tossed the cup and spoon in the trash bin. "I don't have any idea what they mean, or what the device was."

"I think I do. I believe they're infrasounds," Reed offered.

"What the heck are infersounds?" Andy questioned as if Reed were making it up.

"In-FRA-sounds," Z corrected. "I think you're right, Reed."

"Which are?" Andy prodded.

"Sounds we can't hear. Fifteen hertz and less," Reed explained. "There was a man in France..." he paused, before coming up with the man's name. "Gavreau, an engineer. Vladimir Gavreau. He and his team were working on robotics when they started getting sick. But only when inside the building they worked in.

"After some Sherlocking, they found a loose motor mount was pounding out an infrasound beat that the building amplified, even more so when a combination of windows were either opened or closed. They couldn't hear it, but their bodies could."

"This beat was making them sick?" Andy asked, the stone room of his last dream rushing through his thoughts.

Reed nodded. "They discovered it by accident while adjusting their test equipment, in the infrasound range."

"Whoa," Z said in mock surprise. "I'm rolling a joint," then broke out the rolling tray.

"Make it a fat one!" Jointer said.

"When Gavreau and his team discovered what was causing their nausea," Reed went on, "they dropped their robotics study and started toying with infrasounds. On their first try they made a large replica of a gendarme whistle. It killed the technician manning the bellows when they fired it up. Turned his insides into amorphous jelly."

"Pudding," Z clarified.

"These sounds can kill people?" Andy choked.

Reed nodded. "After a few more close calls, the team got a handle on infrasounds, but not before blasting a portion of Marseilles one afternoon." Reed smiled, "They blew out windows for miles.

"At certain frequencies, infrasounds will turn your insides to pudding. At others, it'll cause your body to explode. Some of the infrasound frequencies, for a short duration, can actually feel good. Tesla played with them for a while. Clemens even tried Tesla's machine. But prolonged use will hurt and maim."

"You sound like a government warning," Z interjected.

Reed glanced over to Z, "Shut up and roll." He returned his eyes to Andy. "Gavreau and his team built several machines to generate infrasounds. The pillar in your dream sounds a lot like a description of one of those machines. But there were problems.

"These sounds hug the ground. Although emitted in one direction, they would backtrack or feedback to their origin. Killing those who turned it on. Like that poor technician.

"When they couldn't come up with a way to control it, they quietly put the project to rest."

Andy looked at Z. "I don't know anything about this Gavreau and his sound machines. Why the hell am I dreaming it?"

"Apparently your destiny involves these sounds." It was Jointer. He had moved towards the back while they talked. "This spider sounds like your spirit guide, or something."

"Shut up and find the skins," Z instructed.

Andy turned his gaze out the window, his life taking a weird twist that he seemed to have no control over. But the really funny thing was...he was excited. He felt he finally had a purpose, a reason in life. The fact that he had a spider for a friend was just another bizarre happening he does not understand. Andy wondered if Moses could explain Arabella, or anything else happening to him. Moses' address!

Moments later Andy stuck his hand in the inner pocket of his backpack and pulled out an envelope, a dead insect wrapped in silk stuck to the side. He acknowledged Arabella's meal with a "Tsk", then placed it in the web before returning to his seat.

After a moment of studying the letter that was in the envelope, Andy said, "Forty minutes north of Las Vegas on Highway 95. Five miles north of Indian Springs."

Chapter V

Sixty minutes north on Highway 95 brought Glass Reality to the long driveway of Moses Dark Cloud. Andy said his good-byes and thanks to the band, stepped off the bus and into the Nevada night, Arabella and two joints in his backpack. As the bus pulled away, Andy heard Reed playing the saxophone. Shifting one of the straps of the pack, he started walking up the gully-ridden dirt road.

Twenty minutes later Andy could see the dark silhouette of the shop. Moses' house, smaller than the shop, was between Andy and the shop. At this hour, late evening, Moses was either asleep or in the shop. Andy was betting the shop.

As he got closer, he noticed the door to the house was open and he could see through the doorway into the living room, through the dining area and out the back patio door. The shop light was on.

Andy stopped at the threshold and reached around the door, trying the wall switch for the lights. It was already up, but he flicked it down and up a few times anyway without the desired results. He entered and stumbled through the house to the back door.

"Moses!" he yelled from the backyard, halfway to the shop. The shop was twice as long as the house and taller by half as much.

"Dark Cloud?!" Andy yelled as he reached the building. Then he saw his friend through a window, sitting on a stool in front of a workbench. He stepped up to the window. He was about to knock when he noticed a wire coming from Moses' ear. Headphones. Andy went to the door. He tried the knob and it turned. He pushed the door open.

Moses felt a draft when the shop door opened and spun around on the stool, startled. "Andy!" Moses almost shouted. He reached up and removed the headphones. He was wearing jeans without a belt, a rumpled denim jacket over a red T-shirt, and moccasins that he forgets are on.

"I'd had been here sooner if I didn't have to go through your house in the dark."

"Kitchen light works. The bulbs are above the stove."

"Do your own maintenance. Your an engineer." Andy put his pack down.

Moses stood, the long, denim jacket unfolding until it brushed his ankles, and walked over to his friend. He put his arms around Andy. "It's good to see you, my friend." Moses was four inches shorter than Andy but twenty pounds heavier, lifting Andy off the floor easily.

Andy grunted then reciprocated the hug. "At least you've showered recently."

Moses put Andy down and pushed him away. "You haven't," Moses ribbed, then sat back down. "The light in the bathroom works, too. There's clean towels on the shelf."

"I'm tired. I'll do that in the morning."

"Then you're sleeping outside."

Andy ignored Moses, watching as Arabella crawled out of his backpack. "I brought a friend," he said.

Moses looked behind Andy to the doorway. "Where?"

Andy smiled and pointed to his backpack. "There."

"Hunh?" Moses followed the point to the bag on the floor. "That's all he left you with?"

"Uh-hunh. And I picked up a little hitchhiker."

Arabella was peeking out of the bag, half her body exposed, facing Moses.

"Damn," Moses said, surprised enough to pull his feet off the floor.

Arabella wiggled out of the backpack and sat atop it. She raised her front legs and took in the new locale. She shuddered, then leaped off the pack and scampered out the door, headed for the house. Moses watched her every move.

"That your friend?" he said, looking up at Andy while lowering his feet back to the floor.

Andy laughed. "Yes, a friend."

"She's huge."

"Her name is Arabella. We.." he hesitated, suddenly embarrassed.

"We, what?"

Andy sighed. He and Arabella were going to be there a while, and if she was going to keep showing up in his dreams, he was going to need help understanding what was going on. And Moses should be able to help.

He and Andy had talked before about Navajo beliefs, their legend and lore. Andy remembered that the tales almost always had animals speaking with humans. Maybe there was something to that after all. "She comes to me in my dreams, Moses. She talks to me, shows me things I don't understand." Andy paused and studied Moses' face. Moses wasn't going to laugh, his features were solemn, eyes dark.

"What does she show you?" Moses asked, his voice just above a whisper.

Andy took a seat close to Moses. "I don't understand most of it. I don't know what it means."

Moses shifted positions, remaining silent as Andy continued, the relief of relating the dreams apparent on Andy's face.

Several minutes later, as Andy started to relate what Reed had told him about infrasound, the ground rolled beneath them, causing the building to moan and scream. Moses flung himself over his project. Andy dove under the bench. Light fixtures hanging from the ceiling swayed. Tools and parts randomly fell off the shelves. A few seconds later it was over. The building sighed as the dust settled.

"Damn government." Moses brushed the dust off his shoulders.

"The government caused that?" Andy asked as he crawled out from under the bench. "Ours?"

"Groom Lake is fifty miles north." Moses sat back on the stool. "What do you think?"

"What's Groom Lake?"

"Area 51."

"That, I've heard of. Aren't they suppose to have a Martian spacecraft or something like that."

"Far as I know that's what's causing the earthquakes."

"You can't be serious."

"Hey, I was in that Fly Boy outfit for six years, four of those stationed down at Indian Springs, and I don't know squat about Groom Lake. They could be doing anything out there."

"You don't really think they're causing earthquakes, do you?"

Moses shrugged. "I don't know, Andy," he said dejected. "I find it hard to trust anybody, especially the government."

"Come on, I'll help you clean up."

"Clean up what?"

As they picked up the debris in the shop, Andy continued telling Moses about his dreams and infrasounds.

Frequency Seven

They were sitting in a pair of luxury boardroom chairs Moses had picked up at an Air Force auction by the time Andy finished. Moses had listened attentively through all of it. Then Andy asked, "So, what do you think, Mo'? Am I crazy? Have I lost it?"

"You've never had it," Moses replied. "And you've been crazy since I've known you. Which is why we're friends.

"As for your dreams, I think you should tell grandfather. He'll be able to tell you what it means."

"You mean I finally I get to meet Grey Eagle?"

"Yes. But I need to warn you about him." Moses grabbed Andy's eyes with his, "He doesn't like the White Man."

There was something in Moses' tone that gave Andy the impression that he himself was an exception for Moses. "Are you sure I should talk to him, then?"

"If he's in a good mood."

"Um," Andy hesitated, suddenly unsure of how close they really were. "Um, what?"

"Uh, why doesn't he like...uh, my kind?"

"Besides the obvious, five of them raped and killed his sister when he was nine. She was fourteen."

*   *   *

```
18 Nov 2133 hrs:
    Didn't know they could cause earthquakes. A mild one
that lasted as long as I had the machine on. Obviously the
frequency needs adjusting.
    LG
```

*   *   *

Frequency Seven

An hour after dawn, having slept on a military cot in the shop, Andy awoke to Arabella strutting back and forth across his chest. He raised up to his elbows gently, looking down his nose at the spider. She had stepped down onto his belly and turned to face him. She looked fatter. Bigger.

"Good morning," Andy said to the spider.

Arabella bowed, than ran off his belly and out the door.

"Hmph..?" Andy stood and stretched, then put his boots on before going into the house.

Andy stood in the threshold of the sliding doors looking around the interior of the house and spotted Arabella's web. It was up in the corner to his right, at the end of the wall past the sliding doors. It stretched six feet across, nearly reaching the glass and coming down from the ceiling in the corner four feet. Arabella was near the bottom, wrapping up something big in her silk. Andy took a step closer and leaned towards the web. His eyes widened when he realized what she had in her silk; the tail of the dead mouse dangled freely. "I'm glad you're on my side," he said to her, trying to figure out how the mouse got up into the web. He watched the spider for a few more moments, then turned and yelled for his friend.

"Yeah," came Moses' voice from the front of the house, the door open. A moment later he was in the doorway, taking a step back before saying, "Come on through. I got the jeep all cleaned out. We're ready to go. I was just gonna come wake ya'. Did you get something to eat?"

"No. I'm not hungry. Go where?"

"Grandfather's"

Andy walked through the bungalow to the front door. The long, narrow kitchen was immediately to his left, dishes piled in the single sink. The dining area was to his right, littered with dirty laundry. It was open to the living room, two chairs and a table; clothes draped over both chairs. The bathroom was next to the kitchen, the door open. The only bedroom was after the bathroom, at the front corner of the house.

When Andy turned from closing the front door, he found Moses in the jeep.

"How do you let your house get so bad?" Andy asked as he slid into the passenger seat.

Moses started the engine. As it warmed, he said, "I dunno, Andy. Guess I need a maid." He put the vehicle into gear and they started down the long, rutted driveway. "Did you see your spider?"

Andy nodded. "Did you see what she caught?"

Moses nodded. "I didn't know I had mice."

"What did you expect with the way your place is?"

"Yeah, I guess it is kinda bad."

"When we get back from seeing your grandfather, we're cleaning it up."

"Go ahead. I still got work to do on my latest-" They hit a deep rut just then, the jeep dipping sharply on the drivers side. The rebound forced an "Umph" out of Moses.

"Damn," Moses said when the jeep settled. "That's gotten deeper."

"You've got work to do on what?" Andy demanded.

"A remote-controlled plane."

"They have them. Besides, you have a house that's just going to," Andy let go of his handholds and threw his hands up and out, "burst into flames if you don't get it cleaned up." He quickly returned his hands as they hit another rut. "You hit that one on purpose."

Moses turned to Andy and smiled.

"I'll help," Andy went on, "but it is your house, you're going to clean, too."

Moses agreed, then spent the next two of the three hour drive telling Andy more about his latest project.

*   *   *

Frequency Seven

In a US Geological office near San Diego, California, a mid-level seismologist studies a computer screen. "These P-waves aren't right." She was facing the monitor, but talking to the other person in the room - her supervisor, Stanford Lynn. "The timing of these waves don't look right for an earthquake."

"What? Let me see."

The young seismologist rolled her chair away from her desk without getting up. Lynn stepped in front of the screen and peered intently at the data displayed. "No, that doesn't look right. There's definitely something strange going on there."

"You don't know what it is?"

Lynn was slow to respond. "No. I've never seen anything like this," he lied.

"Do we have anyone that can figure it out?"

"No. Maybe the Berkeley office does." He knew someone, but no one knows where he is.

Lynn studied the screen a few more moments before saying, "I'll be in my office. I'm going to see if I can get a hold of Berkeley."

Minutes later, as the young seismologist continued to study the computer screen, Lynn called out from his office, "Lisa, could you e-mail all that info? Also print out the seismogram so we can fax."

Several more minutes passed while Lisa, the young seismologist, stared at the data on the screen, her mind running possible equations. Then Lynn startled her from behind.

"They can't think of anyone off the top of their heads, either. When they call back, you're gonna have to talk to them. I'm wanted in Oakland. I'm taking the next flight. Maybe between you and Berkeley you'll get this figured out."

Ten minutes later, the faxes had been sent, computer data relayed, possibilities proposed and still, no one at either end of the phone line knew what was going on.

"Do you know anybody that can make heads or tails of this?" the young seismologist asked.

"I use to," came the voice on the other end of the phone. "He left a few years ago. To pursue personal endeavors. Lynn knows him."

"Really? He didn't indicate he knew of anyone."

"That doesn't surprise me. It wasn't one of his better moments."

"What happened?"

"I can't get into that over the phone. But I think I can still locate this doctor who can help you."

"Doctor?"

"Ph. D. Acoustics."

"Do I know her?"

"Him. You might've heard of him. Linus Greene."

"I thought he was dead."

"Not that I know of."

"Can I call him?"

A pause of telephone static. "I'll see what I can do."

"You got my cell number, right?"

"Yup."

"Let me know?"

"Yup."

*   *   *

Two hours through the desert across unpaved roads brought the two men to Grey Eagle's adobe house. A stocky, grey haired man in jeans and light, blue, button-down shirt was watering several short, bushy trees being grown to block the hot, summer sun. His long silver hair was braided into two ponytails that laid over each breast.

Moses stopped the jeep in the shade of some trees further from the house and hopped out. "Good morning, Grandfather."

"Get that White Man off my land," Grey Eagle said, then turned towards his house.

"He's not in a good mood," Andy said to himself.

"It's Andy, Grandfather. My friend," Moses said as he approached the old man. "I've told you about him. He's not like the rest of them. He..he needs to talk to you."

Grey Eagle wiggled his hand at Moses, "I don't care who it is. Those bastards were here again yesterday."

Moses stopped in front of his grandfather, gently grabbing the old man's upper arm. "What did they want, Grandfather?"

"Same crap. They want me to stay off our sacred mountain."

"It's their land now, Grandfather. Government land. You have to accept and respect that fact."

"I cannot respect anything they have done." Grey Eagle looked past Moses to the jeep. "Why must I talk with that White Man?"

"Andy, Grandfather. His name is Andy. Andy Bucansin. He's the one that talks with the Spider Spirit."

Grey Eagle scoured his grandson's face with his eyes, finally snatching Moses' with his austere stare. "Have you spoken with the Spirit?"

"No, Grandfather, but I have seen her. I have felt her power. She is in my home."

Grey Eagle leaned past Moses to again view Andy.

Andy squirmed in his seat, the eyes of the old man burning into him. He could not hear what they were saying and was becoming anxious. And now the old man was glaring at him again.

Grey Eagle looked back to Moses. "Have to admit, he doesn't have an aura of a typical one."

"He's a friend of mine, Grandfather. Do you really think I would have a typical one as a friend?"

Andy stepped out of the door-less vehicle and leaned against it.

Grey Eagle glared at Moses. "You joined their military. You've accepted their ways. Yes, you would."

"I've explained before about the Air Force, Grandfather. And we both know it's one of the few ways for us to be accepted into their world, to make it in their world." Moses waved a hand towards the house, "It's how I bought this land for you."

Grey Eagle turned and started for the house. "It is not their world. It belongs to no one," he said before disappearing into the low dwelling, the blanket covering the doorway waving.

Moses turned to Andy and motioned him over. Andy hesitated, then walked the few yards to Moses.

"He seems upset," Andy said when he reached Moses.

Moses looked to the house, the blanket over the entrance still moving from Grey Eagle's passage, then back at Andy, "Grandfather is fine. He just has to get use to you like I did."

"Like you had to?" Andy muttered. "That puts me at ease."

"Come," Moses said as he headed for the house.

Andy followed, hands in his pants pockets. He put a shoulder into the blanket hanging in the doorway and twisted, moving the blanket from one side as he passed over the threshold.

It was dark inside the earthen home, the air cool and musty. The windows, one in the wall behind him, two in the wall on his left, and one in the wall across from him, materialized first as Andy's eyes adjusted. They were blocked by thick drapery that just covered each window, a thin ribbon of sunlight squeezing around the cloth. Another door, also covered by a blanket, was also in the wall across from him. The fourth wall was to his right and a hallway a little behind him.

Grey Eagle came into focus next, sitting on a couch to his left, behind a coffee table, a single candle burning in the center of the table. In his hands was a long, ceremonial pipe. Grey Eagle lit a match and his front burst with illumination, the room in front of him flashing into Andy's mind like a camera click. The walls were populated with bows, arrows, quivers, dream catchers, blankets, candles and animal skulls. An armless chair made of branches and hide was just to his left, facing the couch. A small table near the kitchenette on the far side made up all the furniture. There was no television, but there was a small boom-box radio on the kitchen table.

Moses was to the left of Grey Eagle. "Sit down, Andy," Moses said.

Andy sat in the hide chair and folded his hands on his lap. Grey Eagle pulled the pipe from his lips and handed it to Andy. Andy, his eyes adjusted to the dimness, glanced to Moses for guidance. Moses nodded.

Andy took the pipe, nodded a 'thanks' to Grey Eagle, then slowly put the mouthpiece to his lips. Grey Eagle and Moses watched intently. Cautiously, the contents unknown, Andy inhaled from the pipe, the bowl a foot away glowing red inside.

The smoke was cool, the taste pleasant, reminding Andy of walking through the woods near his grandparent's farm on a hot, humid, summer afternoon. He filled his lungs with the smoke, then returned the pipe to Grey Eagle, holding his breath as he leaned forward, then back.

Grey Eagle passed the pipe to Moses, then leaned back and exhaled his first draw, the smoke billowing into a mushroom puff over the candle.

Andy, still holding the smoke in his lungs to prolong the absorption, saw an outline of Arabella in the puff over the candle. Astonished, he exhaled the smoke from his lungs into Grey Eagle's puff. The outline of Arabella blew away, but was replaced with a smoky, fuzzy, holographic image of the three of them around a fire pit inside a dark, dome structure. The figures moved and the flames flickered. Andy pulled his gaze from the smoke and looked at the two men on the couch. Grey Eagle was handing the pipe to him.

Andy took the pipe from the old man and again drew deeply from the mouthpiece. He passed the pipe back to Grey Eagle, then put his elbows on his knees, dropped his head between his shoulders, and closed his eyes. A silence grew in his mind during the breathless interlude, a strange feeling of weightlessness came over him as the silence intensified. Time seemed to stop, as too, his heart.

    Andy exhaled...

...and the silence exploded into thunder and pounding horse hoofs. Lightning cracked the darkened scene with a white flash. Andy was on a horse, one of many in a war party. The horse and Andy were bareback, a bow and quiver strung across Andy's back, a spear in his free hand, the other holding the reins. It was late afternoon, dark and raining hard as his group attacked a tiny village by a river.

    Andy watched helpless from the two portholes of the man on the horse as he plunged his lance into a charging warrior. He made one pass through the village shooting arrows into anything that moved and turned around for another pass when an arrow struck him in the chest, pushing him backwards off his horse.

    Andy jerked straight in the chair, snapping his eyes open wide in shock as he grabbed for his chest with both hands. Moses and Grey Eagle continued talking to each other in hushed tones in their native tongue, seemingly oblivious to Andy.

    "Moses," Andy called quietly. "I just-"

    Moses raised a hand, stopping Andy from saying anymore. "Please, in my Grandfather's house you will address me as Dark Cloud," he said, then dropped his hand.

    Andy swallowed, barely keeping himself from running out the door, then restarted. "I..I just saw myself killed, during a raid on a village. An Indian village." Andy paused and inhaled, his being still seemingly detached from his body. "I was a Navajo."

    Grey Eagle reached out with one hand and laid his fingertips on Andy's knee, then closed his eyes.

Andy looked down to his legs and the old man's hand. He did not feel the pressure on his skin, though. The touch went unfelt.

Grey Eagle leaned back straight. "We must go to the hogan now," he said, then blew out the candle as he rose. He walked to the back doorway without another word, flicking that blanket to one side as he passed through, the pipe in his hand.

"Come."

It was Moses. Andy was sure of that, but he sounded as if he was some distance away, not across the room. Then he saw movement in the shadows. Moses had stood.

Andy rose, his legs like rubber. Cautiously he took a step. It felt like his feet were made of cotton. Slowly, Andy followed Moses out the back door, intrigued with the sensations flowing through his body.

When he reached the doorway he flicked the blanket aside and was instantly blinded by the late morning sun. The brilliance forced his eyes shut. Andy kept them closed until he felt he could handle the daylight.

Upon opening his eyes Andy saw a small, dirt-packed dome, about six feet high and fifteen in diameter, just a few yards in front of him. A thin trail of smoke escaped through a small opening in the top. The entrance wasn't on this side, but he could see the top of the door frame on the right side, facing east. He headed for it.

The interior of the hogan was darker than the house. A small, open-pit fire illuminated only the front of Grey Eagle and Moses with just a dusting of light, the rest of the tiny room a hue above black. But he could smell the logs that formed the dome - juniper. The air itself was moist with the earthen floor. Moses motioned with a ghostly wave for Andy to sit opposite the doorway.

Andy shuffled across the dirt floor and took the seat indicated, the dust catching up to him at the fire. Grey Eagle was to his right, Moses across from Grey Eagle.

Grey Eagle leaned to the fire and removed a stick, the far end flaming. He relit the pipe and passed it to Moses, then put the stick back in the fire. Moses inhaled from the pipe, then passed it on to Andy.

Andy, already stoned from the two hits in the house, inhaled without hesitation after taking the pipe. Holding the smoke, he returned the pipe to the old man, who continued the rotation.

Again Andy handed the pipe to Grey Eagle who put it in his lap, who then exhaled over the fire. He saw Andy turn his face away from the smoke. "Watch the smoke, White Man. Blow your smoke here, after Dark Cloud." He pointed just above the flames.

Andy looked to the flames, then to the ground directly in front of himself. He didn't want to see any more. He didn't want to feel what he saw, especially if it was to see himself die.

"The smoke, White Man!" Grey Eagle ordered in a low, stern tone. "You must keep your eyes on the smoke."

Andy looked to Moses as he exhaled his lung full of smoke over the flames. "You must follow Grandfather's instructions," Moses said after catching a breath.

Andy heard the words, but did not see Moses move his lips. He did not see Moses look back to the fire, but Andy was now staring at Moses' left ear. Suddenly, Andy needed to breathe. He faced the fire and exhaled.

The smoke from his lungs struck the smoke hovering over the fire, mushrooming out as if it hit a solid wall. Then it folded over and around the other smoke, enveloping the other two puffs in a transparent, solid sphere. Andy stared, dumbstruck. Marijuana had never done anything like this.

The sphere looked like glass, the smoke still churning inside. As Andy watched, the smoke inside the glass sphere cleared, except at the top. There the smoke became rain clouds, the rain coming down on an Indian war party attacking a village by a river. It was the same scene he had experienced inside the house minutes ago. His stomach twisted into a knot and he wanted to pull his eyes away from the sphere, but could not. Again, he witnessed himself shot with an arrow. Only this time he didn't feel the impact when the arrow struck. Instead the scene inside the sphere vanished, instantly replaced with smoke.

Andy closed his eyes, trying to discern visions from reality when Grey Eagle's mellow voice entered his mind. Grey Eagle was addressing Moses.

"That was many years ago. Our blood is thin in him, now."

"Perhaps, but it is still strong," Moses replied. "The visions are proof of its strength."

Andy heard movement, then felt something near his face. He opened his eyes to the pipe inches from his nose.

"Again," he heard Grey Eagle command. Andy drew again from the pipe, exhaling after Moses. All their smoke penetrating the glass sphere, again churning inside.

As the smoke inside the sphere settled, Arabella materialized. Moments passed into minutes as Arabella and Grey Eagle gazed at one another through the smoke, the crackling of the fire the only sound. Then Grey Eagle reached to the sphere with an index finger extended and burst the glass sphere as if it were a soap bubble.

Instantly, they were in the stone cave from an earlier dream of Andy's. The paintings on the walls were there, the powdered dirt floor cool under his rump. A tall fire burning in the center of the door-less room, the smoke exiting out the hole in the roof, the shadows cast on the walls by those attending flickering with the flames.

Arabella, now larger than any of them, squatted on the east side of the fire, all eight legs on the ground holding her mass slightly above it. The three men filled the other compass points; Grey Eagle on the south side of the fire facing Moses, Andy facing Arabella.

Andy turned to Moses for an explanation, but Moses was looking at his grandfather. Andy looked over to Grey Eagle.

Grey Eagle sat motionless, legs crossed, facing forward with his eyes closed, a look of serenity on his face, apparently oblivious to the move to the cave. Or he had been here before.

Then Arabella's voice reverberated off the stone walls and filled the cave. "Grey Eagle," her voice caused the air to tremble.

Andy felt it as a varying breeze, depending on the syllable spoken. It was the first time Andy had heard her voice through his ears. The perception was odd, disquieting. Her statement and tone to Grey Eagle added to his anxiety. He faced her, the fire dancing in her six eyes.

"Sandpainter with no forgiveness," she called.

Grey Eagle, his eyes still closed, merely nodded in response to Arabella's comment.

Arabella then turned to Andy, "Are you frightened of me?"

Andy shook his head, trying to mask his visible trembling.

Arabella turned to Moses. "Dark Cloud, it is good we meet."

Moses leaned slightly forward, then straightened. "I am honored, Spider Spirit."

"Andrew," Arabella called as she turned back to him.

Andy, still agitated, but calming as time progressed and the spider hadn't devoured anyone, replied with a soft, "Yes?"

"Destiny has brought you and I together for a purpose."

Again, Andy felt, as well as heard the words, the air vibrating in sympathy to the consonants. "What...purpose?" Andy breathed.

"To save the world before it is destroyed."

'Hallucination' flashed through Andy's mind.

"You are here, White Man," Grey Eagle whispered, as if he had heard Andy's thoughts. "As, too, is your Arabella."

"Andrew will realize later, Sandpainter," Arabella stated, lacing Andrew to indicate preference over White Man.

Grey Eagle cringed. He had angered the Spirit with his blind hatred. He dropped his eyes. His grandson liked this Andrew. The Spider Spirit talks with this Andrew. The blood of his people was in this Andrew. He pondered his position while the flames broke the silence. After minutes had passed, Grey Eagle looked up into the spider's eyes. "I will help this Andrew through his journey," he proposed to her. "Anyway I am able."

She nodded, then turned to Andy and barked, "Andrew!"

Andy jerked himself straight.

"Come," she whispered and Andy was wrapped in Arabella's drag line, being pulled through a viscous black . Flute music, long and flowing, rose just above the false static of total silence. The air was moist, cool, and sweet. Andy found himself relaxed, comfortable. His mind was blank, as blank as the surroundings. No thoughts, emotions or desires. He was in bliss. Moments, hours, days passed. He didn't know. He didn't care. He felt...safe.

Then suddenly they quickly slowed and stopped. A jolt of lightning cut through the darkness, the cracking rumble of thunder several seconds behind. Below him, them, was the village attack, just before Andy's predecessor is killed.

Andy watched as he fell backwards off the horse, snapping his neck as he hit the ground. A heartbeat later and what looked to be Moses, rushed by on a charging horse, revenge in his eyes and yell, when he, too, is shot off his horse with an arrow to the chest.

"Holy shit," Andy muttered.

"Shhhhh."

Several more warriors ride by before an older warrior, on foot, paused at the two slain. It was a young Grey Eagle. He pulled the arrows out of the two bodies, and others near-by, before loading his bow and moving on. Then everything went to the now familiar grey cobweb mist.

"Holy shit," Andy repeated. "Do they know this?" he questioned the spider.

"Yes."

Andy unwrapped the last of the dragline from around himself and tossed it towards her. "Do you suck it back in and recycle or litter the place with it?"

The dragline went limp as it fell from her spinnerets. "Make a rope."

"How..." Andy cleared his throat. "How am I suppose to save the world?"

"That is not determined."

"That's a big help."

She turned towards him.

He faced her straight on. "Why me?"

A blue sky opened below them, coming to within inches of Andy's toes. A wooden ship sailed the open ocean, another moments behind, giving chase. The sun past noon several hours now. As he and Arabella descended unseen to the lead vessel, the men on deck came into focus. Andy, another ancestral Andy, stood at the helm, captain of a pirate vessel. A red bandanna was wrapped around his head, reigning in a thick mane of hair. A long, heavy blue coat clung to him as he steered to optimize the wind. When he turned over his shoulder, Andy saw the worry in his face, the fear, the determination.

A cannon blast from beneath Andy's feet rumbled past him and the face on the boat grew more worried. He turned the wheel with the wind, ordering his crew to tighten the sheets as the boat followed the rudder. He glanced back again, in time to see a cannon ball at his face.

Andy jumped as if shocked with a jolt of electricity.

"It's all right," Moses soothed.

Andy opened his eyes to the interior of Grey Eagle's house. His heart was pounding, thumping in his chest, his breath short and deep, a copper tang in his mouth. It had been a hallucination after all. Then Andy passed out again.

Chapter VI

A rut in the road jerked Andy awake. He was strapped into the passenger seat of Moses' jeep. They were on the dirt road that lead away from Grey Eagle's. It was late afternoon, the sun steadily closing the gap to the horizon, translucent clouds on fire in the blue sky.

"How long I been out?" Andy asked, forcing the words through a dry throat.

Moses glanced over to Andy, "Hey, glad to see you back." They hit another rut and Moses turned back to the road, "You were comatose for three hours. Grandfather helped put you in the jeep. We've been traveling," he glanced at the clock in the dash, "for about an hour."

Andy brushed a hand through his hair, "Feels like I've been out three days."

Moses reached behind the seats with his right hand and returned with a small gourd that looked to hold no more than two cups. Rough twine was tied to the neck which lead to a plug in the top. He held the gourd out to Andy, "Here, Grandfather said to give it to you when you awoke. It will help your return."

Andy took the gourd, pulled the plug and smelled the contents. The aroma was light floral. "What is it?"

"Think of it as herbal tea."

Andy watched the road pass beneath them for a while before he sipped from the gourd. He tasted strong chamomile, a hint of sage, and a bitterness he didn't recognize before swallowing the driblet. "Not bad. Want any?"

"That one is yours," Moses said, then pulled out a gourd from beside his seat and held it up to show Andy.

Andy gulped the rest of the liquid from the gourd, quenching his thirst, and starting a surge of energy that seemed to emanate from his stomach, flowing through his blood, the current steadily increasing. He reinstalled the plug into the neck of the now empty gourd and placed it on the floorboards between his feet, then sat back and watched the sunset get just a little bit closer to the horizon.

Minutes passed before Moses spoke. "Grandfather is concerned about you, Andy."

"Sure he is," Andy said, the disbelief blatant.

"He is. After witnessing the vision from the past, and the scolding from the Spider Spirit, he has rethought his position. He told me before we left that he thinks he could like you."

"The vision from the past? The attack on the village?"

Moses nodded. "The Spider Spirit showed us the rest."

"Explains things, hunh?"

"Yes. It does."

Several miles passed before Andy turned his head to Moses and asked, "What did we smoke?"

Moses shrugged, "With Grandfather it could be anything: Peyote, Datura, Cannabis, things neither of us have heard of, or a combination of any or all of the above."

"Yeah, but what did *we* smoke?" Andy reiterated.

Moses was silent as he drove and thought. After only a moment he said, "Judging by the effects, I have no idea."

"I'm not going to have flashbacks or anything like that, am I?"

Moses shrugged. "No. You can only go with Grandfather."

"You say it like we went someplace this afternoon. It was mass hypnosis, that's all."

Moses kept his eyes on the tracks of the road, "Your spirit did go someplace, Andy. An out of body experience. You went to visit the Spider Spirit," Moses turned to Andy to add, "You call her Arabella." He looked back to the road and turned on the headlights.

Things started to make sense now, even if only a little. If this spirit thing is true, then the dreams he has been having are visions. Attempts from the other side to forewarn about a coming catastrophe that he is suppose to prevent. To save the world. But how? And from what, exactly?

This was just crazy. It made no sense. Why him? He had no special training. He didn't have a hero complex. Hell, right now he wasn't even sure whether what was going on was real or some elaborate dream. Maybe he had an automobile accident and is lying in a coma in some hospital.

Moses started downshifting and applying brake. Andy looked out the windshield and saw the highway just ahead.

*   *   *

The next day the two friends spent all morning cleaning Moses' house. Now early afternoon, they were in the shop, discussing Moses' project. Andy stood over the electronics bench, Moses beside him. He was looking at Moses' latest attempt at financial independence.

"So, what is this thing?" Andy asked.

"It's a remote-controlled airplane."

"So. That's not new. My neighbor had one when I was a kid."

"You watch a monitor and fly it by video camera. It's solar powered. You can fly as long as there's sun. Two hours on battery."

"Besides, it's not for sale. This is mine. I haven't figured anything out yet for my big invention. Kinda stumped."

Andy stepped to the bench and looked at the half-finished model. "Won't fly without skin." He turned it around and studied it from all angles. "The design looks good. But it won't fly without skin."

"Do I look like an idiot?"

Andy moved to reply and was cut off.

"Don't answer that. Of course it needs skin. It's just now ready for it. I timed it perfect."

Andy put the model back on the bench. "I suppose that means my arrival."

Moses nodded.

"You just use me, then kick me out when you're through."

"I bet you don't stay longer than a week after getting your check."

Andy smiled. "I better get going on this thing's skin then. Hunh?"

Moses slid back off the stool. "Let me show you where the metal working portion of this facility is."

"Finally, the tour."

"Shut up."

* * *

Over the next several days, Andy helped Moses finish his contraption. Moses tweaked the electronics, fine tuning both the plane and controller while Andy worked on the fuselage. Arabella left for a day during that week, placing an egg sack in her web upon her return.

Consumed in his work at Moses', Andy rationalized the incident at

Grey Eagle's. After all, it was only a hallucination. Perhaps it had been stress all along. He hadn't been visited in his dreams by Arabella since his arrival, other than at Grey Eagle's. Nor had he heard from Tabitha. Yes, that was it: his truck, possessions, means for making a living, all stolen. That would stress out anyone. Moses had seen the stress, and that's why they went to see Grey Eagle. He still talked to Arabella as if she were a pet, waving at her as he passed the web, but no longer did he believe he ever conversed with her.

"You ready?" Andy called over to Moses.

"I think so," Moses said as he turned away from the table and started for the electronics bench. "We'll take it for a quick spin. Then celebrate."

Andy remembered the two joints Glass Reality had given him. They were still in his backpack. "Hey, I've got a couple joints I picked up on the road. We can start the celebration with those."

Moses stared at Andy. "I thought you quit the wacky-weed?"

"After that stuff at your grandfathers, a joint ain't nothing but illegal."

"That's all it's ever been," Moses quipped.

Andy shrugged. "I got 'em from my last ride."

Moses nodded. "It's Holy Smoke. It's a shame your grandfather's prohibit it."

"That's the reason I quit. I didn't want to go to jail."

"You got nothing to worry about out here. The only Fuzz that comes by are going by."

They stepped outside and Andy put the model plane on the ground.

Moses flicked a switch at the top of the controller, then pushed a lever forward. Nothing happened. He looked over his shoulder, "Did you turn it on?"

Andy dropped his eyes to the ground and stepped over to the plane, tilted it, slid the switch on the side, then stepped back behind Moses. "It's on."

Moses pushed the lever again and the plane puttered to a start, then crawled forward. He pulled back on the joystick and it lifted into the air. He did a few quick maneuvers, then said, "Let's get over to the monitor."

Frequency Seven

Andy turned on the monitor, then twisted it so they both could watch. The image appeared within seconds, clear and in color. "Cool," Andy said.

"Way cool." Moses sat down in the chair and started flying while viewing the monitor. "I'd say it's time to break out the wacky-tobacky."

*　　*　　*

"Doctor Greene?"

"Yes," came the timid reply. Then, more forceful, "Who's this?"

"My name's Lisa Patrick. I'm a seismologist with the 'Survey."

"I have nothing to say to you."

"Please, Doctor Greene, don't hang up. We...we have an anomaly with a recent temblor near you."

Linus' mind began to spin. Did they know he caused it? How did they find out? Why then were they calling to tell him about it? "Yeah. So. Why bother me?"

"Your research into this area. You're considered an expert. You come highly recommended from Berkley as the only one who could figure this out."

"You are... who?"

"Lisa Patrick. Seismologist with the United States Geological Sur.."

"I know who the 'Survey is."

"This is my third year."

Third year? She didn't know who he was. "Berkley? Who? Everyone thought I was crazy when I worked for the 'Survey."

"That's not the impression I got."

"You sure you have the right Greene?"

"Doctor Linus Greene. PhD in acoustics. Expanded the work of Love and Strutt, and gave us AST, Acoustical Signature Tracking.

"Stanford Lynn thinks highly of you, too."

"No he doesn't."

There was a moment of silence. Linus was ready to hang up when Patrick spoke.

"I found the anomaly using your formulas. It's in the P-waves. There's a harmonic that suggests it caused the temblor, not the other way around."

"I'm flattered. But nothing can cause a quake. Except the Earth herself."

"But Doctor Greene, the evidence is there in the seismograms. I checked and re-checked my calculations. So did Mr. Lynn."

"It's an anomaly. Like you said."

"I'll be there tonight. My flight leaves soon."

"Where? Here?"

"I'll be staying in Beatty with a friend. I'm bringing equipment to research this irregularity further."

"That's not necessary. It's like you said, an anomaly. A fluke. Probably caused by the rock structure in the area. There's different densities around here. Really screws with the readings."

"Too late. The flight's been booked, bags packed, friend notified, the rental is idling. Where can we meet tomorrow?"

He did not need this. He would have never thought that his own research would come back on him this way. If she comes out with the proper equipment, she could figure out what he was doing. If he was leaving signatures with each test, with enough data they could pinpoint his location to within fifty yards. "You really don't need to come. I can get a hold of the necessary equipment and run your tests. I can e-mail the resu..."

"I gotta go. The car's here to pick me up. I'll call you tomorrow. Bye." Click.

Linus stood there, dumbfounded. Everything had suddenly changed. His timetable was useless. Further testing put on hold. A monkey-wrench named Lisa Patrick had just been thrown into his machinery.

He would have to work around her. He would have to feed her bogus, but believable reasons for the irregularity. Then get her on a plane back to

Frequency Seven

California and get on with his work. She would hear about him later.

*   *   *

Moses sat in the recliner, fully reclined. Andy sat in the short, lime-green, swivel chair. The small, round table between them.

"Think you can sleep in this thing?" Moses patted the arms of the recliner. "It'll be warmer in here."

"I'd rather have a hammock, but it'll work," Andy replied, holding his hand out for the joint.

Moses handed the joint to Andy. "Use Arabella's web for a hammock."

Andy inhaled, then tilted his head back until it rested on the back of the low chair, eyes to the ceiling. Moments later he let out the smoke, his eyes closing and his arm falling towards Moses, the joint between his fingers. "It'd probably hold me."

Moses, giggling from his own remark, saw Andy's arm in his peripheral vision. When he looked over at Andy, he bellowed with laughter. Besides Andy having slid down in the chair, his head on the back of the chair, looking up, his mouth was wide open with the tip of his tongue at the corner nearest Moses.

Andy jerked at Moses' outburst, pushing himself back into the chair, snapping his neck straight and turning to Moses. "What?" he coughed.

Andy's 'What?' just made things worse. Moses laughed even harder, causing him to choke.

Andy looked at Moses, bewildered. "You okay, Bro'?" Andy asked after Moses coughed and gagged.

"I'm(sniff), fine. Just don't say anything else." He rose and started for the kitchen. "I need some water."

"At least you're out of the recliner. I'm going to sleep." Andy put the joint in the ashtray on the table before climbing into the chair.

"Want a blankie?" Moses said in a high-pitched falsetto, then again broke into laughter as he walked into the kitchen.

"No," came a soft, slow whisper from Andy.

When Moses returned, Andy was asleep. He retrieved a pillow and blanket from the closet and placed the pillow under Andy's head, then covered him.

"Sleep well, my friend," Moses said. Before turning off the light, he glanced at the web and Arabella. She had moved the mouse to the top of the web and was feeding on it. "Catch 'em all," he whispered to the spider.

Andy opened his eyes and found himself laying flat on his back in a web, the strands as thick as an ocean liner's mooring lines. They were opal silver, looking as if a thin veil of silk had been wrapped around a two inch glass rod. The sky above him was dark blue, possessing a quality of depth that gave the impression he was looking into a gel. There was no sun, yet it was bright as a Nevada noon.

Grabbing the strands on either side, Andy pulled himself to an upright position, then scooted to the closest corner, legs dangling through the web. The web stretched in all directions, curving downward at the horizon. Then he heard waves breaking on a beach nearby and looked down. His knuckles turned white as he squeezed the web tighter. He was looking down on clouds.

Beneath the clouds was an unfamiliar shoreline, water to his heels, terra firma off his toes, too far away to discern details smaller than a river. The breakers he had heard were but thin, white lines appearing and disappearing at the waters edge. But he had heard the waves crashing as if he were standing on the beach getting his feet wet. Then he heard a series of waves breaking again, just as loud as before. He shook his head at the paradox, then realized he was back in the realm of Arabella and nothing was going to make much sense.

Andy sat straight and looked around again, twisting at the waist to see behind him. He was alone. The dark, blue gel overhead acting as a low ceiling, the web the floor, the scene below surreal.

Below was a planet, alive and blue. He wondered if it was Earth. It had to be Earth. He wasn't far enough away to see a recognizable coast, but the swirling clouds and probable road was enough for him. It was Earth. Andy slid his hands forward on the web and leaned inches closer to the sight below, then whispered, "Arabella?"

The web trembled on his right and Andy snapped that way, expecting to see Arabella, big as ever, strutting across the web towards him. There was nothing but empty space between the web and the blue gel ceiling. Then Andy felt air moving on his back and calves, like a pulsating breeze. In the process of twisting further to the right to see behind, Arabella's voice breathed inside his head,

"Good, you noticed."

He finished his turn. Arabella was right behind him, as big as a dump truck. Then, with a subtle swiftness unbefitting her size, Arabella moved in front of him without causing a stir in the air or a tremble on the web.

He turned and faced her. "The breeze?" he asked, clarifying what he was suppose to have noticed.

"Yes, you noticed the direction in which it came. The next time you feel the breeze, it will not be me."

"What?"

"It will be the whisper of Hell." Arabella then began to shimmer and vibrate. Horizontal waves undulated her form, as if she were standing over a flame, then she was gone. All within the space of a breath.

Andy blinked, then scanned the web again. "Arabella?" No answer. He was alone again. He crossed his ankles and swung his feet as he gazed downward, wondering what was to happen next. Seconds slid into minutes, his mind racing with wonder and awe. *She is such a wonderful planet. Giving plenty of fresh water and food and air. Home.*

After several moments Andy had the distinct notion that the ground below was passing by, rotating. He stopped swinging his feet and watched. The motion below continued, the ground traveling from left to right on a diagonal.

Frequency Seven

Yes, home.

"It is the Mother," a familiar voice filled Andy's mind. He twisted to the right.

"Tabitha!" Andy burst, surprised at his excitement to see her, the fact that she hovered waist high to the web not registering.

"Lonely?" Tabitha said sweetly, concerned.

"Ever since I stopped breast feeding."

Tabitha smiled and drifted closer to him. "Yes, I miss it, too." She held out her hand to him, "Come."

Andy laid two fingers in her palm, sliding off the web without question as he muttered, "That was suppose to be funny."

"You forget who I am. I know what lies beneath your words." She held on to him gently as he too hovered, slowly drifting below the web.

"Maybe you can explain them to me someday."

"Perhaps." She leaned to her right and they were suddenly moving.

It was then Andy noticed they were floating, flying, soaring beneath the web, above the clouds. Andy was slightly trailing Tabitha as she pulled him along. His hair was streaming back flat against his scalp, hers fluttered as if in a light breeze. They were headed for barren ground below on a slight angle. Behind them was the great expanse of water, the web ticking by in a climbing rhythm overhead. Andy stared in awe at the terrain below. He squeezed Tabitha's hand a little tighter.

Tabitha, returning the squeeze, looked back at Andy. "Everything's going to be fine," she whispered into his mind, then squeezed his hand again to confirm it.

"Can you tell me what's happening?" Andy yelled against the wind.

"I am." She sharpened their descent, pulling him with her.

Andy's eyes began to water from the rush of wind, tears streaming across his temples and into his ears. He shut his eyes to stem the flow. He opened his mouth and the wind stole his breath. He tugged at Tabitha's hand, but she continued the descent without falter. Then suddenly he was jerked upright and placed gently but firmly on the ground. He opened his eyes.

They stood on course, sandy soil. Open land with low, rocky dunes surrounded them. Sparse, thin vegetation and plenty of heat. The sun was directly overhead, their shadows small pools of grey cowering by their feet. The sky a bright blue. A front of clouds was poised between them and the horizon to the rear, else it was empty blue, and no web.

"Why did you call Earth the Mother?"

"Because you are born of her; you are sustained by her; you could not exist without her. What would you call her?"

"Home."

"Come," Tabitha gently commanded, then tugged at his hand.

Andy stepped up beside Tabitha and scanned the horizon. "Where are we?"

"Here."

"Where is here?"

"Where we are."

"That's not an answer. What is the name of this place?"

"Earth."

"Oh, jeez. Where on Earth?"

Tabitha stopped and turned to Andy. "Here, silly." She pulled at his hand, "Come on, its just a little ways." She pointed to the top of the dune they were ascending, "Over that rise."

When they crested the dune moments later Tabitha stopped and turned to Andy. "She's not a god, you know."

"Who?"

"Arabella. She is a spirit. An ancient spirit with wisdom and power, but not a god." She stretched up to Andy on her toes, wiggling a finger for him to meet her. He bent down to her and she whispered into his ear, "There are no gods."

Andy nodded, confident he was dreaming.

"Look," Tabitha instructed, pointing down the other side of the dune. Not more than forty yards down and a hundred out was a small town. Population maybe fifty. It was quiet. Too quiet. It appeared deserted. "Come," she suggested.

Andy followed Tabitha down the dune and into the township. There were three adobe buildings: a gas station, a souvenir shop, and a restaurant. All the other buildings were trailers; from fourteen foot travel trailers to large double-wide mobile homes. All of it look like it had been there centuries.

And it smelled. Really bad. Then they came across the first remains.

The person had been sitting in a wooden chair by the restaurant. Now, the shirt was draped over the seat, hanging down to the ground from the front. Carpenter jeans, socks and shoes were piled on the sidewalk beneath the shirt. Deflated skin was inside the clothes, a grey-pink ooze covering both.

"Wha...?" Andy managed to stammer.

"Hell's whisper, Andy. Hell's whisper."

Infrasounds. Andy knew she meant infrasounds. "Is everyone like this?"

"Yes."

Chapter VII

"Thanks, Grandma. That gives me something to think about." Andy was sitting in the swivel chair, awake only minutes, his shoes and shirt still off. Moses was in the kitchen starting coffee.

"It sounds like it could get dangerous," she said.

"I'll be careful. But it does sound like fate, or destiny. I thought that only happened in stories."

"Depending on how this turns out, they could be telling stories about you."

"Don't blow this out of proportion, now. It's not that important."

"It very well could be. Right now it's important enough that you think you're talking with a spider. You cover your butt, young man."

"Yes, ma'am. I'll be careful." He couldn't believe it. She thinks he has been picked to save the world. She even had a dream about it, she said. He was going to need to think about this a bit more. "Now, how are you?"

He could hear her sigh. "I'm just fine," she finally said. Andy could hear the look his grandfather was getting about then. "Just a little sore in the chest. Your grandfather won't admit it, but he's been going to bed with a woody every night since I've been back."

Andy slid out of the chair laughing, flopping butt first onto the floor, the receiver behind his head on the cushion.

"Andrew?" Andy heard his grandmother call over the phone. "You there, Andrew? Andrew!?"

Andy picked up the receiver as he climbed back into the chair, "Sorry, Grandma. I dropped the phone. What did you say after Grandpa's woo.." Andy sputtered out a giggle.

"Andrew Bucansin. You grow up right now and stop that snickering." Then Grandma did it. "You have them, too."

"Grandmother!" Andy exclaimed in mock shock. "I only have the one."

This remark sent his grandmother into snorting laughter. Moments later Andy's grandfather was on the other end of the telephone.

"Okay, Boy. What did you say to her? She's going to rip 'er stitches. Pro'bly drop them sacks right out on the floor."

Andy couldn't help it, his grandfather was serious. Andy slid out of the chair again, dropping the receiver on the floor. His own laughter keeping him helpless on the floor.

Moses came out of the kitchen to investigate the commotion. He saw Andy on the floor trying to stop laughing, the receiver beside the chair. Moses picked up the receiver, "Hello?"

"That you, Moses?"

"Walter?"

"Yeah. What the hell is that boy doing?"

"Um," Moses looked to the floor. "Trying to stop laughing. What'd you say that was so funny?"

"How the hell do I know? He gonna be okay?"

Moses looked again at Andy, who was getting control, slowly. "Yeah, he'll be okay. Want to wait for him?"

"Nah. He'll just start in again. I don't know what he finds so funny."

"Neither do I, Walter. You take care now. I'll have him back to you by spring."

"Watch over him for me, will ya', Moses. I know he's a grown man, but no one should go it alone."

"He's being well taken care of, Walter. Stay warm."

Moses followed the cord back to the rest of the telephone and hung up the receiver, then turned to Andy. "You gonna live?"

Andy was on his hands and knees, his head down, breathing hard. "Uh-hunh." Andy took a few more deep breaths. "Gramps just says some of the funniest things. So does Grandma." Andy nearly broke into another chorus of laughter thinking about the telephone conversation, but caught a grip on it quickly. He stood, staring at Moses, smiling. His eyes were watered and his face red. He wiped at the tears. "Ya' gotta love 'em for it," he said, then started for the back door. "Let's go play with the toy."

"It's not a toy," Moses called after him. "I'm going to use it to see inside Groom Lake," he added when he had caught up with Andy outside.

Andy felt a pulsating breeze just before the ground began to move, rolling under their feet like a waterbed. The breeze continued as long as the quake. The same breeze from his last dream.

"Fucking government and their blessed testing!" Moses yelled as he surfed the rolling ground, both buildings creaking mercilessly.

"It's not the government," Andy said, more to himself than to his friend as he rocked on the same ground. He was looking southwest, the direction he had felt the pulsating breeze come.

When the motion stopped seconds later, Moses asked, "How would you know?"

Andy turned to Moses. "You didn't feel it, did you?" Andy asked.

"Feel what? The ground moving? Of course I felt it." Moses leaned a little closer to Andy, peering into his eyes. "Did you take a few tokes this morning?"

"Tsk. No." Andy rolled his eyes. "You didn't feel that breeze during the shaking?" Andy restated his question. "It came in from the west. Southwest. Just before the quake hit." Andy squeezed his eyes shut, putting a thumb and finger to his temples.

Moses steadied his pale friend with a hand around Andy's bicep. "You okay, Bro'?"

"Yeah," Andy said as he lowered his hand from his face.

The two men looked at each other for a moment. Moses' face held concern for his friend. Andy's held terror.

"Color's coming back to your face," Moses said, then released his grip on his houseguest and stepped back.

Andy turned back to the west, staring at the horizon.

"What are you looking at?" Moses asked.

"What's that way?" Andy answered, the soles of his feet numb, a twang of hopelessness trying to spark into life.

"Not much. A ranch or two. Desert. Rocks. An abandoned missile silo. Mercury is fifteen miles up the road. Amargossa Valley thirty-five. Beatty sixty-five. Why?"

"Whatever caused that earthquake came from that direction." He pointed just south of west.

"How do you know?"

Andy turned his head to Moses and said with a smirk, "A little spider told me."

"Did she tell you where exactly, then?"

Andy had lost the smirk. "No. Just how to feel it. And it's scaring me shitless." The last dream becoming vivid, the images surreal, the melted bodies haunting.

"Mind telling me what this is about?"

Andy shrugged. "I wish I knew. All I know is that a cement tower can somehow bring a city down without any noise. And somehow I feel a breeze when that happens." He looked to the ground, "I felt that breeze before the earthquake hit."

"Are you sure? I didn't feel any thing."

"Arabella showed me the breeze. She said it was the whisper of Hell," Andy said quietly, Reed's lecture on infrasounds playing through his thoughts. "Infrasounds." He returned his gaze west, a fear of the unknown smoldering.

"Your dreams?" Moses asked, a concern in his eyes as he looked at his friend.

"Yes, my dreams. Had another one last night."

"They have you terrified, don't they?"

Andy looked at Moses, "I don't know how to tell you what she showed me."

"What was it?"

Andy looked to the west again. He sighed, then turned back to Moses. "What if," his eyes darted to the ground, then back to Moses. "What if I didn't go through with this? What if I stopped looking for the source of that breeze?"

Moses studied Andy's eyes for a moment, then shrugged. "I don't know. Perhaps your spider could find someone else to carry on. Maybe the world will end if she doesn't." Moses shrugged again, "I don't know. I do know that you will regret it for the rest of your life."

Andy dropped his eyes, then looked west. Moses was right, he would hate himself if he didn't go on. Yet he was now to believe that he was led there by events supposedly orchestrated by a ghost of a giant spider so he could feel that breeze. So he could track down this 'Linus' and stop him from doing whatever he's doing. How was he suppose to do that? Under what authority? The Spider Spirit said so? He twisted his body and faced Moses, "You know, if he tuned that thing to the right frequency he could kill us where we stand and we wouldn't even know what hit us. Suddenly, all your organs shut down all at once. A pressure builds, but death is so quick all you feel is a snug squeeze of your skin. It's a quite peaceful way to go, just ghastly as hell to see the results.

"And the worst of it is? There's no defense. No warning. It just happens. Almost like being bombed. But we can't hear these sounds, there's no plane engine noise, no whistle, nothing of a warning. Just bam, you crumble on the spot.

"That ground roll we just rode could have been the frequency to kill us."

Moses now looked terrified. "Thanks, Bro'. For explaining that. I feel much better now."

Andy looked into Moses eyes. "I can see that."

Moses was gazing southwest, past Andy. Death could always come at anytime, but to think that somewhere out there was someone who could push a button and kill hundreds, thousands, everybody, on whatever whim they might have? That was enough to get him wondering about all the religions and how none of them saw this one. Technology had it's good points, but it also had some very, very bad points. This was a bad point.

* * *

```
23 Nov 0947 hrs:
Getting closer to the frequency. Directional control
improving. Seismologist Patrick called right after the
test. She didn't have her equipment setup. She wants to
meet. At Mercury. Assess the damage. Damn nuisance.

    LG
```

* * *

As they walked through the shop door, they heard a news flash on the radio. "...reports are just coming in. It seems Mercury was hit with a small earthquake. Minor damage being reported so far. People are being taken to local hospitals from a general sensation of feeling ill. No one was injured during the temblor by falling debris. People are experiencing dizziness, nausea, difficulty in breathing, extreme weakness. This could be from a ruptured gas line, one official suggested. Information is still sketchy. We will keep you updated as the reports comes in..."

Twenty minutes later Moses and Andy were at the edge of the driveway in the jeep. A Highway Patrol sped by in front of them, the lights flashing, the siren wailing, headed west at high speed.

"That way Mercury?" Andy pointed after the patrol car.

Moses nodded, then turned right onto the highway, the patrol car already disappearing over the hill.

"So," Moses started after shifting into final gear, "what are we looking for?"

"A little cement tower. A fifty-foot antennae. I guy with a megaphone. I have no idea."

"Great," Moses said. There was no anger in his voice, just exasperation. "I have work to do and you have me driving around looking for no idea." He turned and looked at Andy, "What are we doing out here?" he asked in a manner befitting a concerned friend.

Andy looked from Moses to the floorboards. "I don't know, but I just couldn't sit back there and do nothing after feeling where it came from. There has to be something out here. Something for me to find." He looked back to the floor. "Why else am I having these dreams?"

"I believe you, Bro'." Moses leaned over the steering wheel and scanned the barren terrain ahead of them, "But if there is something out there, it's buried."

They drove in silence, listening to the news reports about the quake damage in Mercury. Several homes were destroyed, but no lives lost or serious injuries. Moses watched the road, thinking while driving. Several more patrol cars passed within minutes of each other before they were again alone on the highway. Andy scanned both sides of the road, then informed Moses. "I bet what we felt was residual of whatever hit Mercury."

"What? Like an aftershock."

"No. More like bleed-over. He aimed at Mercury and we felt what went astray."

"It wasn't infrasounds though. The radio said no one was hurt."

"He must be testing frequencies."

"I hope they adjust it wrong each time."

A few miles later Andy asked Moses to stop the jeep.

"What for?" Moses responded. "See something?" They had just crested the hill that leads down to Mercury, just under seven miles away.

"Maybe. Back up."

Moses put it in reverse and eased off the clutch, backing on the shoulder of the road. A few moments later Andy again told him to stop the jeep. "There," Andy pointed to the horizon. "That stump."

Moses stared, squinted, even got out his binoculars from behind the seat. He saw short shrubs and rocks, but couldn't see any stump. "Where?"

"Just wait." Andy jumped from the jeep, quickly checked the road, then scurried across it. He hopped the three strand barbed-wire fence on the other side and headed across the land. He moved slowly through the lunar-like landscape, the tumbleweeds-to-be giving the barren, rugged terrain extra obstacles. He walked with his head down, sidestepping the desert bushes as he slowly receded from Moses. A few yards in he paused behind a large shrub.

Moses was wondering if something was there, the stump, a snake, when he saw Andy motion as if zipping his fly. He suddenly understood. Suddenly, he had to go himself. He stepped out of the jeep and around to the far side.

A car approaching at high speed caused Moses to turn to the highway.

Seconds later a Highway Patrol car whizzed by with only lights flashing. When it had passed Moses turned back to Andy, only to discover he couldn't see him anymore. He climbed back in the jeep and set the binoculars on the seat, then turned the radio on and listened to the news.

Fifteen minutes later, on the rising desert breeze, Moses faintly heard his name being called. He turned the radio off, then turned to his left and scanned the area for Andy. Instantly he saw his friend waving his arms on a distant rise, silhouetted against the bright horizon. Moses snatched the binoculars and quickly focused in on Andy. He was standing on a stump. What looked like a perfectly round, stump. He grabbed the canteen from the back and started the long hike to Andy, muttering, "This had better be good."

Andy stood on top of a concrete bunker, watching the silhouette of Moses approach. He watched for several minutes, then surveyed the surrounding area. They were out here in the middle of nowhere; twenty miles from Indian Springs and four or five from Mercury. How was this thing being controlled? He couldn't see any wires, obviously no antennae. And who controlled it? He looked up.

White scratches had been scraped into the blue tundra of the sky, remnants of a panther wind. The air was warming, the sun closing in on noon. Andy was excited. He was on an adventure. He knew he shouldn't be excited, that he should be afraid, terrified. If this thing he was standing on came back on, chances were that they would die. Yet, he felt confident that they were safe.

"What the hell is that?" Moses asked when he reached Andy, handing him the canteen.

Andy sat on the stub of concrete nestled in a group of small boulders. It rose out of the ground two feet, inches taller than the surrounding rocks. It was three feet in diameter with two rows of square horns embedded flush on one side, facing northwest.

"This, my good friend, is what causes cities to crumble," Andy patted the side of the miniature, cement pillbox. "According to someone I met recently, this is a Frequency Seven machine. And is it sump'n." Andy opened the canteen and began to drink. It had all come together when he saw the concrete block. When he climbed atop it, everything Reed had told him on the bus about infrasounds whizzed by like a film on fast-forward. He had been hesitant to look into the mouth of the horns, but inspected the entire structure while waiting for Moses.

Andy hung his legs over the side. "Now, I'm just guessing," Andy warned, "but I'd say the sounds are causing the earthquakes. Maybe it's the amplitude, maybe the frequency. But I guarantee infrasounds caused the earthquake." Andy looked to the ground while Moses absorbed infrasounds.

"How fast can you rig up a scanner?" Andy asked after a moment.

"To scan for what?" Moses ferreted.

"The radio signal they're using to control this bunker..speaker..thing," Andy explained. "Unless he's using underground cable, which would mean he'd have to be close. But I doubt it, too easily traced. He has to be using a transmitter of some kind to turn it on and off."

"Uh," Moses started, scanning the surroundings. "Where's the antennae?"

Andy shrugged. "Maybe it's satellite. Maybe the antennae's built in."

"Possible. To both," Moses responded, then started thinking about the circuitry required for a scanner.

Andy waited impatiently for Moses to give him a time frame. "Well, how long?"

Moses shrugged. "I could have something crude by tomorrow."

"What about working?"

"Um, day after tomorrow."

"We'll set it on top this thing, and when it's signaled, we'll know the direction it came from and search in that direction. But we don't want to be around when it turns on."

Moses shook his head. "What if it's satellite?"

"I doubt it. If this is government, and I don't think it is, then they'd want it to stay secret. Bouncing a signal off any satellite to control something like this is too risky. I bet the antennae is built in. Coiled, so it appears taller."

"I know what coiling does. We should be able to come up with a range of frequencies we can scan for based on this things dimensions."

"Gotta a tape measure?"

"In the jeep."

They stared at each other for a moment before Moses stuck a hand into his pants pocket. "Heads or tails?"

"Tails."

* * *

They stopped at the road block and identified themselves. The credentials held by Patrick got them in with a "Ma'am" from the sentry.

"That's impressive," Linus remarked as they headed into town.

"What is?"

"The way they let us in. What do your papers say?"

"The usual, I guess. Lynn had 'em made up. This is my first field trip since college."

Linus knew her papers weren't the usual. They didn't even ask her about him. Something wasn't right. "What college did you go to?"

"UCLA. You?"

"Hunh. Uh, East coast."

"What? Are you ashamed or something? What school?"

"MIT."

"Oh."

"And Princeton. Before MIT."

"Double, oh."

"For knowing so much about my work, you know very little about me."

"All there is to find about you is your work. There's no information on your background, your schools, nothing. Going through college I figured you were dead. Then when they told me they had your number I begged them to let me call."

"Does this mean your a fan?" his voice held a subtle hue of disdain. He turned to her, looking at her as a woman, not a scientist. She was plain looking and wore no make-up. A slight chest and long, strawberry-brown hair would draw men to her. She was okay looking. But she had to have a decent head on her shoulders if she understood and used his formulas. That would turn a lot of men away. He could like her. He wondered if he could trust her. But why were they simply waved in?

"I'm impressed with your work. I think I can improve on it, though. I mean, if that's all right?"

Improve on his work? "Improve? What do you mean?"

"I'm pretty sure I can pinpoint the epicenter with one station. By combining your research into P-waves and your AST, I'm certain I can find an epicenter with one seismograph."

Find an epicenter with one 'graph. And they thought he was crazy. "Consult me before publishing?"

"Deal."

It was then he noticed the soldier on the curb, talking into a microphone while staring directly at them. He had seen one earlier, but thought nothing of it. Seeing this second one though made it click. They were watching him.

"Why is there nothing about your background Doctor Greene? I even Googled you and came up only with your seismic work."

Does he tell her that he and the 'Survey had a falling out? That he didn't believe they should be helping the FBI conduct it's microwave tests. That he had fought against the GWEN towers and failed. He did succeed in getting himself labeled, however. Depending who you talked to, he was a liberal, a communist, or just simply a wuss. "Let's just say that the 'Survey and I didn't see eye-to-eye on things. And, since they are the government, they have the power, and the ability, to make me disappear."

"Our government wouldn't do something like that."

"You got another explanation? I even put up my own website, only to have it inaccessible in a day."

"You must have really made them angry for them to wipe away your past."

"Oh, they got rid of my future, too. I haven't published anything since before leaving the 'Survey. I did get a large separation package that's let me stay out of employment, but my work is going unnoticed, wasted."

"Maybe I can help with that."

"How do you mean?"

"When I modify your formulas, I'll give you your credit, and then I can introduce your recent work."

He was going to re-enter the scientific world on the coat tails of a third year seismologist? He would show them another way. "I'll be anxious to see how you pull that off."

They drove in silence a few more blocks before Patrick pulled the SUV to the curb. She put it into Park, but left it running. Two blocks up, Linus watched a soldier reach for his microphone. Paranoid sons-of-bitches. "So, you'll be able to locate the epicenter of what did this?"

Patrick reached behind them to the rear seat and retrieved her camera. "No. I need to have the seismograph record the quake. The aftermath doesn't do me a bit of good."

"Then, why are we here?"

"Lynn is going to e-mail me the seismogram from our office. I think it'll be useless, like the last one. It's just too far away to pick up the subtleties necessary for my calculations. So, I'm going to setup a 'graph."

"Good idea."

Patrick stepped out of the vehicle and started taking pictures of the damage. Wooden structures had collapsed. Adobe buildings cracked. Mobile homes knocked off foundations. The place was a mess. She took seven pictures, then climbed back into the SUV. She put in gear and pulled away from the curb.

"Where are you staying?"

"I'm staying with a friend in Beatty. She has one of those Airstream trailers. Thirty-four foot, I think. It's kinda small, but she's been there six years now."

Linus looked at her crooked. "Airstream?"

"Silver. Rounded corners."

"Oh, yeah. They don't make them any more, do they?"

"Over seventy years. They're an American icon."

"An icon? Whew. Shows how much I get out."

"Want to go for dinner after we're done here?"

He looked her over again. "Dutch?"

She snickered. "Sure. Dutch."

Chapter VIII

The next morning, while Moses tinkered with circuit boards and electronic chips inside the shop, he listened to Wally Hancock on an AM station. A news bulletin interrupted the monologue, informing listeners of a freak explosion at Amargossa Valley.

Andy was outside behind the shop, staring at the distant mountains, absorbing the site and the sun, when he heard Moses calling. He headed for the front of the building.

"What?" Andy said when he met Moses at the side of the shop.

"They just broke in with news on the radio of Amargossa Valley being hit with something. They said it flattened every building in the city."

Andy's face paled. "I didn't feel anything. No breeze. He's getting better. We gotta tell somebody, Moses. Tell them what we know and what we found." The excitement Andy had felt earlier was now panic. "This has gotten outta hand. We can't do anything about this."

Moses responded calmly, rationally. "Tell who what? That a spider told you that there's a machine that's going to destroy the world with sound waves?

Sound we can't even hear. They'll either think we're crazy, or that we have something to do with it. No. It wouldn't be a good idea."

"Everything's going to be fine." It was Arabella. *"Trust me."*

Andy looked towards the house, then scanned the yard as he turned back to Moses. "You have a point." Moses hadn't heard Arabella. He felt he barely had a grip on himself as it was and that didn't help. "Can I borrow your jeep? I have to go see."

"I'll just drive you."

"No," Andy said quickly. "You need to keep working on that direction finder."

"No problem, Kemosobe. Me work hard. Me no sleep. Me no eat. Me no..."

"Oh, stop it and toss me the keys."

Moses dug into his pants pocket, pulled out his keys and flipped them to Andy. "Put gas in 'er."

*   *   *

Andy turned on the radio when he hit the highway, listening for updates on the earthquake. "...tuned for more updates of the freak temblor that struck Amargossa Valley," came out of the speaker. "Now back to Wally Hancock."

Andy turned Wally down. No reports of injury. It's still early. A Highway Patrol passed him and he focused on driving. He had almost forgotten how much he loved to drive. He missed his truck. He missed driving. The focus on the task. The wandering of the mind as the rest is concerned with the current endeavor. Andy's mind settled on the memory of when he had met the jeep's owner.

They had been at opposite ends of a blackjack table in a small casino in Las Vegas. Andy was losing and was about to walk away when a Caucasian man in a business suit started yelling about the Indian at the end cheating.

Andy had to stay and watch; he knew the gentleman at the other end of the table was not cheating. If anyone was cheating, it was the house.

The dealer, a rookie, asked the man in the suit to "Please quiet down", and told the man in the red shirt and blue jeans to leave the casino. That's when Andy had spoken up.

"Excuse me. Dealer? Excuse me." The dealer looked Andy's way. "I could see the gentleman at the end of the table the entire time and he never cheated. If anybody's cheating, it's the House. I'm down fifty bucks and I've been holding at nineteen."

"You Indian lover. You fucking..." the accuser shook his head. "You realize you're calling me a liar."

"I never said you were a liar. You're simply be mistaken."

"Now you're saying I don't know what I'm doing; what I'm seeing?"

"There just ain't no pleasing you, is there mister?" Then Andy laughed. "Me, Indian lover. We're all human. Though half the time you won't get me to admit it. Not with ones like you walking around."

The accuser made a quick move towards Andy.

Moses, who had been enjoying the display, was ready and caught the man in the suit before he got two inches off the stool, setting him back down rather roughly. The accuser tried to turn to Moses to attack him, but Moses kept him off balance the few moments until casino security arrived. They cuffed the man in the suit, then gave Andy a stern looking over.

Moses Dark Cloud was a regular customer back then, and a regular winner. "He's all right, Steve," he told the security guard. "You should have heard him tell that guy off. He's cool."

After security escorted the man in cuffs to the back, they thanked Moses, then apologized for the trouble. Over drinks later, Andy and Moses exchanged histories and became friends.

His thoughts rambled after that, to times with Moses, his grandparents, and what little he had of his parents.

Frequency Seven

Five miles from Amargossa Valley Andy stopped the jeep after cresting a hill. Military trucks obstructed the highway about a mile down the road, faint figures swarmed around the trucks. Andy could see the flashing lights of emergency vehicles, civilian and military, going towards the struck town that sat north of the highway, hidden behind a hill.

"Naturally," Andy said to no one, then turned the jeep around and backtracked. He hoped to find a side road somewhere.

Two miles later Andy saw a road grader, a backhoe and two dump trucks across the lane, on the north side of the highway. Checking for traffic and braking hard, Andy quickly whipped across the opposing lane and through the gap in the fence. As Andy followed a dirt path that led past the construction equipment and up into the rocks, he wished he knew where he was going.

After driving the path for a few minutes, Andy noticed that someone else had passed recently. What vegetation there was had been flattened in the direction he was now going. His stomach tightened a little and he stopped the jeep.

Andy sat there with his arms draped over the steering wheel, his head bent down staring at his knees. Why was he nervous? Nervous? No. Scared? Yes. But frightened of what? The damage to the town had been done. He wasn't doing anything wrong. There wasn't a sign saying he couldn't come this way, and the gate had been open. He was only intending on looking at the town. Whomever was up ahead, if anyone, didn't know his intentions, nor what he knew. What would he say if it were the police, though? The military? Maybe it was just part of the road crew. Maybe they had already left. Maybe's. He had to go look. He had to see the destruction. Andy shifted into first and continued on, stopping again ten minutes later near a dark green pick-up truck. A late Sixties model, it had a white, metal shell rusting to the bed.

Andy stepped out of the jeep and studied the incline of jagged rocks before him. The slope was twenty feet up at a steep angle. Rocks of different sizes jutted out from scattered locations; sand, gravel and tiny plants filling the space in between. Andy put the keys in his pocket, grabbed the binoculars from the back of the jeep and walked over to the pickup truck. The windows on the shell were curtained off, the cab empty and locked. Andy scanned the slope for the driver of the truck, but saw no one. At least it wasn't the police or the military. Andy slung the binocular case over his shoulder and started up the slope. He glanced back at the truck, feeling he had seen it before.

It was a relatively easy climb, the chiseled rocks and tufts of grass gave numerous hand and footholds up the sharp hill. As he climbed closer to the top, Andy could hear the wail of sirens in the distance, and feel the wind that brought them over the ridge. There was also an odor in the air that he couldn't quite make out. The sirens and the smell got stronger as he ascended.

At the top of the flat ridge, the strong wind lifted his hair and rustled his clothes. The odor became recognizable. It was fresh death. Lots of dead bodies for the smell to carry this far that strong. Off to his left several miles was the highway. Boulders, a hundred yards to his right, was the only thing breaking the skyline on the plateau besides him in either direction. No one else was to be seen. Andy removed the binoculars from their case and scanned the terrain directly below him. Nobody. He checked the rocks to his right. Again, no one. Andy turned the glasses to the west, where Amargossa Valley is...was.

The scene from his dream overlaid the magnified sight through the binoculars. The news reports hadn't exaggerated, the town was flattened. Not a building or wall was standing. Smoke and flickers of flame still rose from the rubble.

"Holy fuck!" Andy said as he stared through the glasses, watching the red, blue and yellow lights of emergency vehicles flash to and from the devastation. "How many people?" he muttered to the wind.

"Population was about five thousand," came a male voice from behind Andy. A familiar voice.

Andy spun around, holding the binoculars at his side by the strap, ready to use as a weapon.

Frequency Seven

A man stood several feet away holding a small bore pistol by his waist. It was aimed at Andy's midsection. It was the driver who had abandoned Andy in Wyoming.

"What..?" Andy saw the muzzle blast as the '-t' clicked off his tongue. He heard the shot as his left side, just below his ribs, burst into flames. He spun to his left, facing the decimated town as he grabbed the burning opening, dropping the binoculars. His knees buckled beneath him, the horizon going on a slant before it went dark.

As the shooter stumbled down the hill trying to recall the face of the man he just shot, a spider crawled into Andy's shirt at the collar.

* * *

```
25 Nov 1958 hrs:
    Rumbled Amargossa Valley today. Every building
collapsed. This will not do in Dreamland. Only the
sandmites. Nothing else. What good would the alien
technology be under tons of rubble? I will have to adjust
the frequency.
    Also, I killed a sandmite today. He surprised me
while I was observing the results of my test on Amargossa
Valley. A face to face execution of a sandmite. Rather
disturbing watching someone die up close like that. And, I
think I have seen him before. I believe he is the one I
picked up in Wyoming, on my way back from Toronto.
    Can't wait to hear from Patrick.

    LG
```

Chapter IX

     A flash of lightning jolted Andy awake, the crack of thunder a second later affirming the fact. Exhausted as he felt, the raindrops pelting his face would not allow him to fall back to sleep. He laid on his side, already soaked, the cold just now registering. He opened his eyes to the last of the flames from Amargossa Valley, the flashing lights of emergency vehicles still moving around the flattened town.

     Andy tried to move and barked with pain, the echo sliding into the distance under the rain. His left side had been numb, but now felt on fire, the only warm spot on his body. He dropped his head to the rock with a damp thud. He felt weak, nauseous, fading. He closed his eyes, trying to remember why he was lying on the ground.

     Another bolt of lightning brought the flash of the gunshot back to Andy's memory. Again he saw the face of the man that pulled the trigger. "What was he doing here?" he whispered to the rock. "And why the hell did he shoot me?"

     Moses. He had to get to Moses.

Frequency Seven

It was night. What time though? Without the stars it was impossible to even venture a guess. Now Andy wished he wore a watch. He rolled slowly, gently to his right and pushed himself to his knees, the gunshot wound burning hotter.

The cold rain on his back felt good but did little to quench the burning that was spreading from the hole in his side. Andy inhaled, held it, then stood with a scream that chased his earlier echo. He was up, though. Dizzy and unbalanced, but he was standing. The binoculars on the ground came into focus with another lightning flash. Afraid he would pass out bending down to retrieve them, Andy turned and started for the jeep.

The first step with his left foot nearly sent him into unconsciousness. Each subsequent step sent a shudder of hot pain up and down his left side. By the time Andy made it the short distance to the edge of the slope he was walking in shock, his face pale, eyes glassy. His body was tingling with a prickly heat, yet he focused on staying upright and moving his feet. He started down the hill, the warmth of Moses' home his ultimate goal.

A third of the way down Andy slipped and stumbled, rolling and bouncing off rocks until he hit bottom. He stopped face down next to the left front tire of the jeep, unconscious, blood seeping out the larger exit wound in his back.

A spider crawled from beneath a nearby rock and went under Andy's untucked shirt.

*   *   *

The phone rang again. Again he let it go to the machine. Again, it was seismologist Patrick. Again, she was screaming. Perturbed. "It didn't record a damn thing! Not one single fucking wiggle! What did you do to that machine Doctor Greene? You said you were checking calibration. It didn't record anything! What did you..."

Frequency Seven

Linus snatched up the receiver "I didn't do anything to your blessed machine. I checked calibration and it was good. It didn't need adjusting. You forgot to turn it on."

"How dare you suggest that I did something so lame. You saw me check it. You saw the needles move."

"Yeah. So. You must of hit the off switch when you pulled your hand back. I didn't even touch it. I just looked."

"I would have known if I hit something with my hand, and I can assure you I didn't."

"Not if something else had your attention."

"What? The mess that was left of that town? It was disturbing and difficult to witness, but it didn't affect my judgment."

"I wasn't talking about that."

She paused a moment. "You?"

"Your my biggest and only fan."

"You pompous old fool. I find your work interesting. Incomplete, but interesting. As for you, Doctor Greene, you're too old and a slob."

"I guess this means you don't want me to look at the seismograph."

"Peggy will look at it."

"Peggy? That your friend?"

"She's an electronics technician for the Air Force. She'll fix it."

"Excellent. Well, you call if you need me."

"Don't hold your breath."

*   *   *

The warmth of the morning sun welcomed Andy back to this world. So too, did the burning ache in his side. He pulled himself to his feet with the support of the jeep's fender. He was weak, extremely weak. He looked to the sky. It was still early, the sun had just let go of the horizon. As he climbed into the jeep, holding his right hand over the wound, Andy wondered why he hadn't bled to death. It didn't matter, though. He hadn't and that's what was important. Although he did feel weak enough to answer the eternal mystery at any moment.

Andy turned the ignition key. The engine started without hassle. He only had to hold on for a little while longer, then Moses would take care of him while he went back to sleep.

Sleep. Yes, sleep. Andy felt he could sleep the sleep of a slave. He pushed in the clutch and doubled over in pain, banging his head on the steering wheel. He eased his foot off the pedal, shifted in the seat and tried again. Going slow was bearable. He could get the clutch pedal down. He would need to shift as little as possible. He put it in second and revved the engine as the jeep crawled from a stop. In the opening ahead, Andy turned the jeep around and headed back to the highway. With luck, he will have to shift only once more at the highway. He concentrated on missing the larger ruts, fighting the pain and the desire to pass out. *Just crawl under a thick cobweb blanket in an orb web hammock and sleep as Arabella tended to his wound.*

Andy shook his head and found himself on the highway heading southeast towards Moses'. He had to stop wandering off before he met a pole head on.

"Stop what?" Arabella said from his right.

Andy looked to the passenger seat. Arabella occupied the space, man-size; two legs on the armrest on the door, her head twisted towards him. He turned back to the road before answering.

"What are you doing here?"

"Helping you get home."

"How about spinning up a patch for the hole in my side, then," he let out a short burst of laughter that sent a hot flare up his left side. He fell forward on the steering wheel, causing the vehicle to jerk left. Wincing through clenched teeth Andy pushed himself upright and put the jeep back in the proper lane. The blood from his wound seeped into his pants and squished between his buttocks. He was awake now. He stole a look at the passenger seat - Arabella was gone. He returned his eyes to the road.

The scenery ahead was familiar. It was the western side of the box canyon where Moses lived. Just a few more minutes and he would be safe.

Then his vision fell in on itself; a clear spot down the center of a fuzzy edged blackness. Through the tunnel vision he could see the front of the vehicle and his side of the lane about thousand feet ahead. Andy slowed the jeep, but didn't stop, afraid of bleeding to death if he hesitated. The highway divided and Andy moved to the inside lane, concentrating on the edge of the road, anticipating the turn to Moses'.

He felt weak, extremely sleepy, and was still seeping blood. It was taking forever to come across the turn. He needed to reach the crossover soon. It was still another two miles up a gutted road after reaching the turn off before he could rely on Moses' help. Where was the turn? This was taking too long. Concerned about passing out before reaching Moses, he increased speed until...there!

Andy threw the shifter into neutral, slapped his foot on the brake pedal and cranked the wheel to the left. The jeep bounced on the gravel shoulder, nearly sliding past the median crossover before it jerked onto the short, gravel path. It felt as though a hot rod had been pushed into his side, still trying to burn its way through to the other side. When the jeep was pointing at the driveway on the other side, Andy downshifted to second and floored the gas pedal. The jeep straightened out with a snap and headed across the median, spitting gravel from the tires.

A red car whizzed by the small opening in Andy's sight just before he reached the other lanes. He leaned on the button for the horn to warn any others that might be approaching that he was crossing the road. The front tires hit the shoulder's edge, jerking the jeep up hard. Andy yelped in pain. His hand came off the horn as the rear tires struck the pavement edge.

Frequency Seven

Another horn blared and rubber screamed off cement as a northbound sedan braked and veered to miss Andy. Andy's heart leaped into his throat. That had sounded real close.

When the jeep was on the gravel apron of Moses' driveway Andy eased off the gas, knowing deep ruts were just beyond the short gravel entrance.

The first rut was on the driver's side, causing Andy again to be bounced in his seat. A hot flare went up his side, keeping Andy dazed with pain, but awake. He kept it in second as he leaned to the right in the seat, feet flat on the floor, idle pulling the jeep up the drive. When the burning eased, Andy scooted his right foot and gently pressed on the gas pedal. He had to get to the house. Now!

An excruciating eternity later Andy saw the roof to Moses' shop. He laid on the horn until he saw Moses running from the house towards him. The last Andy saw was himself falling sideways into Moses' arms.

Moses laid Andy on the kitchen table, then gathered items to tend to Andy's wound. He set the items on the counter, then pulled back Andy's shirt and stared at the wound. Covering the hole in the skin was a thick web, damp with blood. Moses gently rolled Andy over to the right and looked at his back. The bullet had gone all the way through, the exit wound covered by the same damp webbing.

"The Spider Spirit is strong with you, my friend," Moses said to the unconscious Andy, laying his friend back flat. "Those web patches and cold night probably saved your life."

Carefully removing the cobweb patches and replacing them with gauze and tape, Moses cleaned and dressed Andy's wounds in silence. Periodically Moses would glance over to Arabella's web. Arabella remained motionless in the center of the web, facing Moses and Andy.

When Andy's wound was dressed, Moses lifted the lighter man with the tenderness of a brother and carried him to the bedroom, laying him down on the bed. Moses then hung a dream catcher above Andy before moving a simple wood chair next to the bed and sitting down.

Minutes later Moses heard a noise in his silent house and looked towards the bedroom door. Arabella stood in the threshold for a moment before darting up the wall. Arabella scurried to the ceiling, crawling cautiously to the dream catcher. She examined it for a moment, then started spinning a web around it. It was almost nine in the morning.

Shortly before noon the phone rang. Moses rose and left the room to answer it. It was Walter.

"We just heard about that town near you. Are you two all right?"

"We're fine, Walter. Andy's taking a nap, right now, though. Want him to call you when he wakes up?"

"No. No, that won't be necessary. Just as long as I know he's okay."

"He is, Walter. I'll tell him you called."

"Thanks, Moses."

When the sun slid behind the western ridge, Moses stirred. He slowly stood, stretched and creaked, his knees popping and back cracking, then went to the bathroom before going into the kitchen.

In the kitchen Moses fussed around the stove, stirring herbs into a pot of hot water. He figured it wouldn't be until sometime tomorrow before Andy would be awake enough to talk, but he hoped he could get some of this tea down his friend's throat.

He was curious as to what had happened. The authorities had to have blocked the roads to Amargossa Valley. Did Andy have a run in with them? But that didn't sound like Andy. An attempted car-jacking? What had happened? The tea was ready.

Moses returned to his bedroom and his patient. Andy responded to the tea with a fit of coughing before waking enough to drink half the cup, then fell back into a deep sleep without saying a word.

Moses sat in the wooden chair and finished the tea as he admired Arabella's web surrounding the dream catcher. She had used the talisman as the

Frequency Seven

center for her web.

* * *

```
26 Nov 2331 hrs:
```
I wait. Impatiently. Seismologist Patrick is making things difficult. If I could just find that sweet frequency. I could hit Beatty. Put that problem to rest. I have but days to find it. Without her finding me.

```
LG
```

Chapter X

The morning sun peeked under the heavy curtains covering the bedroom windows. Moses noticed the change in luminosity and lifted his head. Dawn. He stood, stretched, then went to the window and opened the curtains part way. He returned to the side of the bed and looked at his friend.

Andy's color was better, the dark rings under his eyes were going away. Moses stretched again, looking to the ceiling and Arabella. She dangled from a dragline halfway down to the bed. He stood eye level with the spider.

"Morning," Moses said softly.

Arabella kicked a leg and twisted slowly until her eyes were on Moses, then kicked a leg on the opposite side and spun back to face Andy.

"I'm going to make some tea," Moses said to the spider, then left the room.

Andy stirred, shifting slightly as Moses passed through the threshold. Arabella lowered herself to the bedclothes after Moses was gone. She left herself attached to the dragline.

Andy felt himself being lifted by his abdomen and looked down at himself. He was being pulled up by a silk dragline coming from the hole in his side.

He looked up to see Arabella, larger than himself, using four legs to haul him towards her. He was in the grey void again. Moses' bed and bedroom, minus the roof, was surrounded in the grey below him, the rest of the was house gone.

"You are frightened of me," came her soothing voice in his head.

"I'm dying," Andy replied verbally. He was now within arms reach of her.

"No. Merely sleeping. Healing," she stated.

"But I feel myself slipping away."

"No. Everything's going to be fine. Come. I have something to show you."

Andy was released from the dragline, Arabella vanishing above him as he began to fall. He was apprehensive, expecting to hit the bed any moment. But as seconds turned into minutes and he continued to fall, his apprehension turned to fear. How could Arabella do this to him?

Then suddenly he was in the back of a moving pick-up. The gunshot wound in his side was gone and he was standing, holding on to a roll-bar behind the cab. The grey, misty void was gone. It was night, late, and he faced forward as the early model truck raced along a dirt road.

Andy and the driver of the truck were in a desert. Flat, open land. Sparse, short vegetation. Dark, distant ridges twenty or more miles away. The sky was clear, the stars bright, the full moon casting shadows from behind.

It was when Andy looked from the sky to the road ahead that he felt a jolt. The truck shifted sideways. Andy kept his grip but was slammed into the back of the cab.

He pulled himself back upright and was about to pound on the cab roof when there was an acceleration. He knew it wasn't the truck, it didn't feel right, and the stars..the stars were moving too fast. It was more as if the ground itself were speeding up, the planet herself speeding up. As if spinning faster. But that was...impossible.

Andy held on tighter to the cold metal bar, the fear of not knowing what was happening mixed with the helplessness of not being in control sparked panic. He beat on the roof of the cab with his fist. "Let me drive!" he screamed into the wind. There was no response from the driver. With effort, Andy bent down and looked in the back window at the driver. It was Linus. The marionette!

Andy was stunned. He straightened up, shocked at the situation. Again he was racing along the desert floor, driven somewhere by a puppet. An acceleration, not related to the truck, caused the stars to leave arcs in the night sky. He didn't know where he was or where he was going. It was Arabella's world, but something seemed different. Then he heard the screams. Voices of millions of people dying slow, agonizing deaths. And they sounded close. Andy looked around expecting to see a mass of people, each emitting their own death scream. Instead there was only desert, blurry as it raced by.

Again, Andy slapped on the cab with his palm, this time yelling for the driver to stop. When they caught up and passed the moon a moment later, Andy let go of the roll-bar and fell backwards out of the truck, landing butt first on a barstool, the screams of the masses still in his ears.

He was now in a tavern, which was little more than a large wooden shack, lit by candles on the walls and dangling kerosene lamps from the ceiling.

Andy was at the middle of the bar, the crowd tight around him. He stood on the footrest of the stool, a hand on the bar to steady himself, and raised above the crowd to look around the room. Glass Reality played on a corner stage to his right, oblivious to what was happening around them. People were packed in like cattle waiting for slaughter, all looking up and past him.

Andy turned around to a black and white TV that hung from the wall, to the right of the mirror. Suddenly the voices in Andy's ears went quiet. Glass Reality quit playing. He could hear the newscast crackling out of the blown *speaker.*

"...still gaining speed. Our atmosphere will be torn away if we continue accelerating. We don't have an estimate..."

A voice bellowed from behind, drowning out both the newscast and the screams of millions from outside, "Did you hear? We're all gonna die! Drinks are on me! HAHAHAHAHAHAHAHAHA!"

Andy jerked awake, sitting up quickly, his left side instantly searing with pain as cold sweat dripped off his forehead. His moan of pain was played through a sigh of relief, the burning candles in Moses' bedroom a welcome sight.

"You all right?" Moses asked.

Andy turned his head to his left and tried to talk, but the wound made it difficult to talk and hold himself up. He nodded before easing himself back down. "Bad dream," Andy whispered. His mouth was dry.

Moses looked to the ceiling at the dream catcher. It was suppose to intercept bad dreams.

Andy followed his friend's gaze to the ceiling. He had seen dream catchers before, but this one was huge. The diameter of the circle had to be two feet. Then he saw Arabella's web interwoven through it. The dream catcher was about a third the size, the rest was web. Arabella sat in the center of the dream catcher.

"Appears Arabella likes your dream catcher," Andy said.

"That one is yours," Moses replied.

"Oh? Really? Why is it so big?"

"You have powerful dreams," Moses said with a weak smile.

Andy pushed his head back into the pillow and looked at Arabella. "I'm hungry," he said softly after a moment.

"I'll check our road kill choices," Moses said as he rose to leave.

Andy started to laugh, then winced in pain.

"Sorry," Moses said, then walked out of the room.

Frequency Seven

Andy wondered what the dream meant. The pick-up truck, Linus, the screams of millions, and the racing moon. He would have to discuss the dream with Moses.

*   *   *

```
27 Nov 0756 hrs:
    I hate waiting. I've toyed with the amplitude,
frequency and harmonics. I'm ready to rumble again, as
soon as it's clear. If this next rumble turns out
successful, I can start my acquisitions.
    Have not heard nor seen anything in the news about
the sandmite I shot. Am tempted to return and see if the
body is still there.
    Have not heard from seismologist Patrick, neither.
If I was sure of the frequency, I'd rumble Beatty. End her
interfering.

    LG
```

*   *   *

Andy had finished telling Moses about his recent dream and now waited for a response. He watched Moses' face, trying to read it.

Moses continued to stare at the floor, knowing the dream was a premonition because it had passed the dream catcher. But what was the interpretation? Was it the initial one of Doomsday he felt as Andy related his dream, or the one he tried to conjure up now? Moses closed his eyes as he slowly raised his head. He opened his eyes when his head was level and looked at Andy. He didn't like what he was going to say. His voice was low, coarse, "It sounds like a premonition. A premonition for the end of the world."

The gravity of his statement struck Andy with a nauseating feeling. He stared at his friend. "You really think it means the world is going to end?" Andy's disbelief held a hint of hope. Hope that Moses was wrong. Hope that the dream was wrong.

Moses shrugged. "Perhaps. Or it could just be your brain catching up on all that's happened to you."

"That's no help. Which is it? Am I going crazy or have I been picked to save the world by a spider?"

"Considering the consequences, I hope you're nuts."

"What the hell is that suppose to mean? Ass."

"If this guy can destroy the world with this thing and you don't stop him..."

Andy cut him off. "Okay. Okay. I see your point."

"But if you're not crazy, I sure hope the spider made the right choice."

"Now there's a confidence builder. Shithead."

"I'm just telling you as I see it. And I see getting shot turns you into a real jerk."

"Piss off. How am I suppose to stop this?"

Moses nodded at Andy's wound. "Your not stopping anything like that. Hey, what are you doing? Lay back down."

Andy had his hands behind him on the mattress, arms extended and elbows locked. "Help me up."

"Lay down. You're starting to bleed."

Andy fell back to the pillow, the pain from the wound only a numbness but he was weak. "You're wrong, Moses. You have to be wrong. The dream was just something from my subconscious. It has nothing to do with the future or the end of the world. It was just a dream."

"If it was just a dream," Moses looked to the dream catcher, "that would have stopped it from reaching you. It was a premonition. A glimpse at the future. A possible future. Perhaps, I hope."

Andy looked to the ceiling then back to Moses. "I don't mean to be rude, but that's just a silly Indian myth."

"And your god isn't silly?" Moses retaliated. "Just because the White Man made him up doesn't make him anymore real."

"I'm sorry, Moses. I..I guess I don't like the idea of the world coming to an end."

"Nor I, but the future is not certain. There still is a chance. But we must be careful."

"Careful of what?"

"Not to cause the end of the world." Moses glanced to Andy's wound. "Although yours almost did."

Andy laid a hand on his wound. "Yeah. I owe him for this."

"Be careful. Revenge is not a worthy goal."

"Now enough about dreams and visions. Who shot you and why?"

"Remember that lift I told you about in Wyoming? That real short one before the band picked me up?"

Moses nodded.

"I'm certain it was him."

*   *   *

```
27 Nov 1255 hrs:
    His vehicle was gone, so I climbed the ridge just in
case. He wasn't there. I followed the blood trail back to
where his vehicle was parked. I am assuming I only wounded
him and he drove himself somewhere. Did he recognize me?
Does he live in Beatty?

    LG
```

Frequency Seven

*   *   *

Over the next three days, between fiddling with the electronics and calibration and tweaking the software, Linus tailed and noted the movements of Lisa Patrick. All three days she was back in Beatty, at the trailer, by half past three in the afternoon. Her friend Peggy would show up within the next ten to thirty minutes.

*   *   *

Four days after being shot, in the late afternoon, while Andy was in the backyard splayed out in a lounge chair soaking up the last of winter vitamin-D for the day, a news bulletin over the portable radio next to him reported a localized, seismic phenomenon near Beatty, Nevada. The newscaster explained that although all the buildings were still standing, it appeared that the populace were all dead.

"Moses!" Andy yelled toward the open shop door.

"I heard," Moses said from inside the shop. A moment later he appeared in the doorway. "Think it's those infrasounds of yours?"

Andy nodded. "But we need to make sure."

"How?"

"We'll have to visit Beatty and see."

"You sure?"

"Yeah. Why wouldn't I be?"

Moses stepped over to Andy and put a hand on his shoulder. "I wouldn't blame you for wanting to quit. Getting shot is traumatic. Let the authorities sort it out."

"I don't trust the authorities to do anything right. Besides, they're likely to find this weapon and put it to use, instead of destroying it. Remember, they're the ones that thought up nuclear weapons." Andy put his hand over the gunshot wound. "As for this, it's no big thing.

"Is the scanner ready?"

Moses nodded. "Too late though."

"They'll be another."

"I hope not."

"We'll set it up on the way back from Beatty."

*   *   *

```
1 Dec 1643 hrs:
    Oh the excitement, the elation. The rumble at Beatty
was successful. The reports are still coming in, but so
far not one survivor has been found, and the buildings
still stand! I called seismologist Patrick and no one
answered. If the authorities find no one alive, I'll
rumble Dreamland and change the world.

    LG
```
*   *   *

Seventy minutes later, as Andy and Moses approached the crest of a ridge via a dirt road, they heard the following over the radio:

"...Due to the recent devastation at Amargossa Valley resources are limited for the search and rescue at Beatty. Volunteers are not being accepted though, due to the unknown nature of the problem. The government does not want to risk any more civilian casualties. The limited resources will mean that the operation in Beatty will take longer. How much longer the authorities won't say..."

This bit of news came as a relief to Andy and Moses. It would be easier sneaking around with fewer military personnel there. The cover of darkness was going to help, too.

Moses stopped the jeep and the two men climbed the short ascent to the top of the ridge as the sun slipped behind the horizon, the few clouds a burnt orange. They huddled behind a large rock at the edge of the plateau. Down the slope and across two miles of flat was Beatty.

"You bring the binoculars?" Andy asked.

"Don't have any anymore."

"Oh yeah. Sorry."

"Forget it."

"You ready?"

"Me? I'm not the one who was shot." Moses peeked around the rock. "Yeah. Let's go."

Moses led the way as he and Andy made it down the gentle slope to the flat.

After they made the flat, Moses asked, "How you feeling?"

"Not bad. My side doesn't hurt any worse than if I were catching rays in your backyard," he lied.

They picked their way through the scattered desert shrubs, the wails of sirens heard between crunching footfalls. They consumed sixty minutes before coming upon a thirty-four foot silver trailer a quarter-mile outside town. The corners were rounded to decrease wind resistance, but it was obvious this camper hadn't seen the highway in years.

Canvas awnings stretched from the front and rear doors. At the edge of the rear awning a rusting barbecue grill stood in the center of a semi-circle of four green, plastic lawn chairs. In front, two garbage cans, one bright silver, the other dented and rusty, stood guard at the end of the driveway near this end of the trailer. A small, red, box-like car sat in the driveway, an SUV parked on the side of the drive in front. Lights were on inside, and what could be movement at one of the windows.

Andy and Moses stopped and squatted behind a large bush fifty yards from the trailer, watching it and the surrounding area for several minutes.

On the far side of town they could see emergency lights and the headlights of the search vehicles, the howl of the sirens skirting through the sparse low buildings and mobile homes of Beatty. Satisfied they were alone, they moved to the trailer.

As they reached the point to go either left or right, Moses suggested, "Let's try the back."

"Any particular reason?"

Moses pointed to the door. Andy leaned to his right. On the top step, lying across the threshold, a white, medium-sized dog lay dead.

As they walked to the back of the trailer, both men noticed the eerie silence. A silence broken only by their own footfalls crunching on the coarse sand and the haunting wail of sirens.

Moments later they could hear voices in the trailer. They weren't right though. It took a few seconds before they realized it was the television. Moses stepped over the dog to enter the trailer. Andy stopped and stared at the dead animal.

The carcass was thin and sunken, as if it had been laying in the heat for days, not hours. Fluid of some kind had come out of every orifice of the animal. The stairs were covered with the mixture of ooze. There was a pool on the gravel underneath, undisturbed.

Andy bypassed the steps and the dog with no eyes with a giant step directly into the trailer. The dog on the steps was little warning for what they were going to find inside.

Andy stepped into the dining area and a wall of stench. Death, alive and aromatic, snuffed his will to breathe. He put his sleeve to his mouth and nose and looked around.

Directly ahead Moses knelt by a body in front of a leather recliner. The rest of the little square room was to the right. A TV against the wall opposite the recliner, on. A game show flickering in the surreal living room: the movement from outside. On the far wall was the front door, shut. Down the hall off Andy's right were two doors; one on the left, one at the end.

A half-wall behind the recliner separated the living room from the kitchen on the left. A wooden support column sliced the open space above the wall at the end.

Andy pulled a bandanna from a pants pocket and held it over his nose and mouth before he moved beside Moses and looked at the body.

It was female. The body was face down in a folded mass. The lower legs were under the thighs and hips while the upper torso was leaned forward until the face was touching the floor, almost as if she were praying. But it wasn't right, the back wasn't arched. The body looked deflated, just like the dog's. The clothes draped over the mass as if they were a pile of dirty laundry. A large puddle of fluid similar to that by the dog surrounded the body: blood, feces, urine and mucus all mixed together in a pool of thick, stagnant ooze. A pinkish-grey goo had bled out of every orifice of the body.

Andy knelt beside Moses. "Infrasound," he said through the kerchief with a confidence as though he had seen this before, images from his dream surfacing. He felt as though he would vomit any time.

Moses turned his head towards Andy. He too, had a kerchief over his mouth. "Air Force." He reached passed Andy and grabbed the TV remote of the arm of the chair and hit the mute button. "See the uniform. Looks like she just got home. We have to stop these men," he said. He turned back to the body, placing the remote by it. "I figure she was sitting in the recliner watching TV when the sounds hit. Then she just slid out off the chair and folded up on the floor."

"I guess we have definitive proof that watching TV is bad for you," Andy said.

"Funny," Moses criticized.

"Just trying not to puke. Man, does she stink."

Moses studied the corpse, examining the puddle of ooze before turning to Andy and saying, "It looks like bone fragments in this shit."

"The sounds must have pulverized the bones as well. It all came out with the blood," Andy guessed, then gagged. "This is getting to me. Let's get out of here."

"Not until we check for others."

"What? We know what did this."

"In case somebody survived."

"Nobody survived. Trust me. Besides, the Army..."

"Air Force."

"The military will be here soon and they can take care of any survivors. Now let's go."

Moses stood. "I'll check the back of the trailer, you check the kitchen," he said as he headed for the hallway. He was at the first door before Andy could stand.

Andy watched Moses disappear through the doorway before stepping around into the kitchen. There he found another woman on the floor, dead. She lay face up by the sink, her strawberry-brown hair splayed out like a fan. An apron was around her waist and yellow, rubber gloves on her hands. She too, had died due to exposure to infrasounds. Only Andy could see her face, sunken beyond the point of recognition. The eyes had burst and the pink-grey ooze had pooled in the depression of the sockets and spilled over. Now Andy vomited, onto the feet and legs of the corpse before him.

Andy wiped his mouth and chin with his bandanna and checked to see if Moses had heard. After a moment Moses came out of the first door and went in the last one at the end of the hall.

Slowly, against his will, Andy stepped over to the body, bent down, and grabbed her pinkie. He lifted the arm and the pudding-like contents inside the skin rolled down to the shoulder. He dropped the arm and it slapped the linoleum like raw meat. He jerked to a stand and his head spun. He grabbed for something sturdy, his hand finding the base of the wooden column.

*   *   *

"Johnson!"

"Yes, sir?"

"See those two."

The young agent looked across the open expanse, easily spotting Andy and Moses heading away. "Yes, sir."

"I want to know who they are before we're finished here tonight."

"Yes, sir."

*   *   *

Moses sat with his hands on the steering wheel as he faced the windshield. "Is there any defense against these sounds?"

"None that I'm aware of. From what I know, they can pass through anything." Andy paused, causing Moses to look at him. Andy made eye contact, then added, "And the real bitch of it is, you don't even know it's coming."

Moses turned back to the windshield "Maybe that's for the best," he said, then started the engine and headed for the road.

After they pulled onto the highway, Andy said over the rush of air, "Something tells me he's ready for his big play now."

"He?"

"He, they, whoever."

"What makes you think they're going to do something else?"

"First, Mercury. Then Amargossa Valley but it destroyed the buildings. And now Beatty, death without destruction. I think he's ready for the big one."

Moses was quiet as he thought Andy's statement through. After a moment he postulated, "'Vegas?"

"Maybe."

They drove several minutes further before Moses asked, "You think he's got a hand-held version of this thing, or do you think he'll do to Vegas what he did to Beatty?"

Andy only shrugged. "We don't even know for sure that that's where he's going to hit next. And if we're there when he does we'll be as dead as everybody else. And who are we going to warn? Telling them what? Besides, 'Vegas has a steady stream of cars heading to it. He'd have to stop all that."

"My, aren't we the asshole today."

"I'm sor..Piss off. How am I gonna stop this thing if I don't know where it is?" Andy slammed his fist into the dash. "I wish I knew what the fuck to do."

"All we can do is what we can, but we have to *do* what we can."

"Profound," Andy mocked.

"It happens sometimes," Moses kidded. "And don't slug my jeep again."

"I'm sorry, Mo'. I guess being picked to save the world has me feeling like I got the weight of the world on my shoulders."

"Oh, now that's profound."

"Just drive."

Half way home after setting the scanner, Andy turned to Moses. "I gotta piss. Pull over."

Moses nodded. He looked at Andy, leaving his eyes off the road as he spoke, "How are you gonna stop a man, Andy? You ever kill anyone?" Moses lifted his foot off the accelerator as he waited for Andy's response.

Andy looked at Moses. "No, I've never killed anyone." Moses turned off the road, the jeep losing speed, as Andy continued. "I had to kill a dying calf once; a litter of infected kittens and the mother, but never a human," Andy said, then went quiet as he stared out the side. The urgency of urination was getting worse. He looked to Moses, "Who says I have to kill anyone anyway?"

"How else you going to stop whoever is doing this?" Moses said, frustrated with it all.

"How about getting him arrested?" Andy offered.

"What if he's working for the government?" Moses countered. "Some secret weapon or something?"

Andy cocked his head to one side, "Then why ain't he at Area Fifty-One?"

"More top secret than Groom Lake?" Moses mused, leaning on the steering wheel and looking at the scenery through the windshield. "Do wish I knew what was going on. I hate this mys..."

"Would you stop the jeep?!" Andy commanded. "I gotta piss."

Moses hit the brakes, stopping the jeep with a dip. "Sorry."

Chapter XI

"What the hell are we doing with all this clandestine crap?"

The were in the penthouse suite on the top floor of the best hotel/casino in town. The men talking are equals, but in different departments. They are senior managers. One is with the FBI, the other is with the CIA.

"What's your problem?"

"What does this guy have that we want?"

"He's figured out how to control infrasounds. And until we know who he's working with, we watch. Right now all we have is a couple of nosy neighbors and a dead seismologist."

"Infra-what?"

"Infrasounds. Below fifteen hertz. We can't hear it, but our bodies do. We did a little research on them back in the 'Seventies. We gave it up when we couldn't control their direction. We figured if we couldn't figure it out, no one could. The French gave it a shot a decade before we did. They couldn't control it either."

"How do we know Greene is using infrasounds?"

"Lynn said there was a signature on the seismogram that proved it was induced with infrasounds. A frequency right around twelve hertz."

"Lynn? Who's she?"

"Lynn's a he. Stanford Lynn, head seismologist in San Diego. He's the one that got that dead digger to get Greene to show his face."

"What's he know about this Greene?"

"Lynn studied his work. He thinks Greene quit to research deeper into infrasounds, but Greene didn't quit. He found out about GWEN, ELF, and HAARP. Made a big stink about it. Threatened to go to the papers. The FBI paid him to stay quiet. Nobody's heard from him until now."

"GWEN? ELF? Oh," he pseudo-slapped his own forehead. "Mind control."

"Among other things."

"What's so great about these infrasounds?"

"They can be lethal."

"So can GWEN."

"Not on this scale. We could crank it up on an enemy, wipe out an entire town, then go in with wet/dry vac's and clean it all up."

"You'll have to enlighten me on that. I have no idea what you're talking about."

"Infrasounds can cause your organs to liquefy. You crank up the amplitude, fine tune the frequency, and it all comes out their mouths and ass. The bone is pulverized with a harmonic. Really does a number."

*   *   *

A week had passed since the 'rumble' at Beatty. The sun setting. Andy and Moses killed time in the shop as they waited for a radio signal to trigger the scanner. Andy swept the shop floor while Moses read a newspaper he had picked up at Indian Springs earlier that day.

Andy passed Moses and glanced at the back of the paper. On it was an advertisement for Glass Reality. Andy stopped and pulled the paper out of Moses' hand to read the ad.

"Sure, be my guest," Moses said, then folded his arms across his chest and stared at the back of the paper.

"I am." Andy folded the paper and held it up for Moses to see. "Check this out: The band that I hitched a ride with is playing in 'Vegas this week."

"So?"

"We might need some help."

"Finally! You think we need we help." Moses paused. "What makes you think this band will help?"

Andy shrugged. "Maybe they won't, but they know about infrasounds. Maybe they can tell us more. Besides, I'd like to see them perform."

"What about this?" Moses waved his hand by the monitor.

Andy looked at the monitor while he thought. After several moments he asked, "Can you rig it so it'll page you when it turns on?"

"Sure," Moses nodded. "You really like this band."

"Yes, I do." Andy handed the paper back to Moses.

"What if..you know," Moses said as he took the paper back and looked at the ad.

Andy knew Moses meant the possibility of infrasounds being blasted at the city. "You don't have to go."

"What? And miss hearing *the band*? What have you been smoking? Besides, I haven't been to 'Vegas in months." Moses looked over the advertisement again. "We can see 'em tonight, if we hurry."

"What about the pager?"

"If we hurry," Moses repeated, then stood and went to the workbench and started punching on the computer keyboard. "Grab that transmitter board there, will ya'?" he said over his shoulder.

Frequency Seven

*   *   *

Andy was impressed with the nightclub. It wasn't all that big in size, but it was sure to get the band some exposure. Over half of the tables were occupied, and there were more people waiting to come in. Andy and Moses were seated three tables from the stage, below the edge of a large, crystal chandelier. It hung in front of the stage, suspended fifteen feet from the floor on a chrome plated chain attached through the ceiling. The walls were decorated with sofa-size land- and seascapes. A short hallway connected it to the casino next door.

A conservatively dressed couple were seated behind Andy and Moses. In the few minutes before the show started, careful observation would lead one to believe that these two were observing the two in front of them.

As glasses of water were placed in front of Moses and Andy, the lights dimmed as the band walked on stage. Andy pointed out each band member to Moses, explaining who each was as he knew them. That took two songs. The rest of the show was spent sipping sodas and enjoying the music. Glass Reality played for sixty-five minutes, each song leading into the next.

At the end of the set, Jointer introduced the band to the audience, then announced they were taking a break. A minute after the band had left the stage, Andy heard Thorton's voice.

"Andy?! It is you."

Andy twisted to the right and saw Thorton approaching. He stood to greet Thorton, extending his hand.

The couple behind them both whispered into their wrists.

Thorton grabbed Andy's hand and yanked Andy to him, hugging Andy hard enough to force an "Umph" out of him.

When Thorton let go, Andy said, "You guys(cough), sound great. No wonder you're playing here."

"We were lucky to get this gig. Our new agent is a wizard."

"I dunno," Andy refuted. "I think you guys sound pretty good."

"Well, thanks, Dude. I..we, really appreciate that."

"Thorton, this is Moses Dark Cloud," Andy said as he put a hand on Moses' shoulder.

Moses stood and offered his hand to Thorton.

Thorton shook it without hesitation. "Good to meet you, Moses. You the one we left him with, right?"

"I'm the one. You guys do sound good."

"Thanks."

"How is everybody?" Andy asked.

"Fine. Z is moody as always, but that's nothing new."

"Sit down," Moses offered.

"I can't. I gotta get back," Thorton leaned close to Andy's ear and whispered, "I want some of the joint before we go back on stage." Then, at normal volume, "Can ya' stay? We'll come sit with you after the show. This is our last set for the night. I know Z wants to see you. I think he missed you."

"How sweet," Moses teased.

"Shut up," Andy ordered politely.

"I better get back. You two play nice."

The next forty minutes went quickly, the songs again leading into the next, either lyrically or melodically. It was five past midnight when they stopped for the night. At twelve-twenty the members of Glass Reality joined Andy and Moses at their table. After introductions and compliments on the band's sound, Andy immediately asked Reed about infrasounds.

Again, the couple behind them whispered into their wrists.

"I've told you 'bout everything I know, Andy," Reed explained.

"Can they cause earthquakes?"

Reed thought a moment, his eyes floating up as if reading cue cards above Andy's head. "I don't know. If the frequency was right, perhaps. Earthquakes do produce them," Reed shrugged. "They hug the ground, traveling along it for miles. And they go through the Earth, the harder the rock the faster.

"Sound travels through the air at roughly seven hundred miles an hour. Through sea water at over three thousand miles per hour, and through the soil, around seven thousand. Hard rock, ten to fifteen thousand miles per hour."

"What about killing people and leaving buildings?"

Reed and the other members of the band stared at Andy.

"It's a joke, right?" Jointer tried.

Z, looking at Jointer, said, "He's talking about Beatty," then looked to Andy. Andy nodded. Z turned back to Reed and prodded, "Can they?"

"At the right frequency they can kill. I told you about that technician," Reed replied, then noticed that everyone wanted to know more. He leaned forward, putting his elbows on the table. "There's creatures in the ocean that use infrasounds to stun their dinner," he lectured. "Giraffes and elephants use them to communicate. It's in some thunder. When your windows in your house rattle, that's infrasound. Pipe organs produce them too. The lowest note ever built was around nine hertz. Church windows have been broken and church goers made ill."

Andy recalled the music the driver in Wyoming was listening to. It had been pipe organs. The nausea he had felt must have been caused by the music. That's why the sick feeling became worse when the volume was turned up.

"The French did a lot research with infrasounds. Mostly that Gavreau guy I mentioned before. Most of their results are classified. However, seven hertz is suppose to be the deadly frequency. The one that turns your insides to jelly."

"Frequency Seven, the Death Ray," Jointer hissed as if in a B-movie.

"Shut up, Stoner," Reed scolded, then added, "Besides being unable to come up with a defense against the sounds, they couldn't control it directionally. It has a tendency to spread out."

"What's up?" Z asked Andy.

Andy looked at Moses.

Moses shrugged, then nodded and said, "All they can do is laugh."

Andy told Glass Reality about the earthquakes, the bunker, Amargossa Valley, Beatty. He did not tell them the details of Beatty, nor about getting shot.

"So why are you after him?" Z asked Andy.

Andy glanced over to Moses, who just rolled his eyes. What was Andy to say; that he had been picked by a spider to save the world from destruction? No. It just sounded too silly.

"Yeah," Kip added, "why haven't you gone to the cops?"

"And tell them what?" Moses proposed. "That Andy is having dreams about the cause of the recent earthquakes."

"I do find it a little hard to believe," Thorton threw out.

"I don't blame you," Andy said. "But if you saw what we saw at Beatty, you'd believe me."

"What did you see?" Kip asked.

Andy turned to Kip, but before he could say anything, the pager on Moses' belt went off. Andy quickly turned to Moses. Moses was staring back.

"What is it?" Z asked.

Moses nodded to Andy. Andy turned back to the band and said, "You guys wanna follow us? We might need your help."

The band eyed each other for a moment. Finally Z nodded.

"Do we have time to pack up the bus?" Reed asked Andy.

"How long will it take?" Moses asked.

"Ten minutes. Tops," Z stated. "All we gotta do is batten down."

"We'll be out front. We're in a jeep."

*   *   *

Andy scanned the radio dial, searching for information as to what had occurred as they waited for the band. Andy and Moses didn't speak, both fearing the worse. All they knew was that the bunker had been signaled and the Frequency Seven machine activated. Just past a country music station, Andy stopped the dial at voices.

"...details are still sketchy. We do know that whatever happened at Beatty earlier this week has just occurred at Indian Springs. Authorities are en route and are asking everyone to stay away from the area..."

Andy turned the volume down. "Did they say Indian Springs?"

"Shit! Home," Moses voiced his fear.

"Area Fifty-One," Andy realized with a whisper.

When music came back on, Andy asked Moses, "Think we'll be able to get past?"

"One way or the other."

They listened to more news, the details vague and sketchy. No mention of how wide an area was hit.

Glass Reality's bus pulled up behind and to the left of the jeep. Moses checked traffic, waved at Jointer behind the wheel, then pulled out into the lane and headed to Highway 95. A dark green SUV pulled in two vehicles behind the bus.

As they passed Las Vegas city limits, they caught a news report: "...and officials are urging everyone to stay home. Highway 95 North has been shut down south of Indian Springs. Highway 95 South has been shut down north of Beatty. Intersta..."

The authorities had Highway 95 blocked off before you could see Indian Springs. The two vehicle caravan had to backtrack to a side road that came back to the highway a mile or so before Moses' home, a detour that added an extra thirty minutes to their trip.

The dark green SUV pulled up to the road block and made their report. "We can't follow them down that road. They'll know they're being followed."

"They're gonna know shortly after getting back, anyway," the agent in charge said. "Ames and Pinkney never made it back. We're pretty sure they were at Dark Cloud's house when this thing hit and that the house was in range. They don't answer the radio or their cell phones. And we don't have enough people to go look for them." He looked to the ground that was lit by headlights and flashing red and blue emergency lights. Another vehicle was approaching. The agent twisted his head to watch. It was a civilian. On vacation by the looks of the rack on the roof. He raised his head. "This thing has gotten way out of hand. Greene raided the base. Groom lake base. He fucking raided Area Fifty-One. Everybody out there is nothing but a pool of flesh." He pulled out a cigarette and lit it. "Did you bug the jeep?"

"Yes, sir."

*   *   *

Moses entered his house and flicked on the light switch as he stepped in. Andy held the screen door open as Glass Reality followed Moses inside. When Andy entered he found Moses and the band staring up at Arabella's web.

Arabella's egg sack was ruptured, a milky white, honey-like substance dripping from the sack. Her eggs were gone. Arabella? Andy's eyes scanned the web, looking for the yellow and black spider. In the upper, right corner of the web he saw a splotch. Goo was hanging from the web, wall and ceiling. Two of Arabella's legs dangled loosely from the goo on the web.

"Guess we were lucky we weren't home," Andy said quietly.

"Re-eal lucky," Moses replied as he stared at a corpse of a stranger. He had turned to head for the shop and saw the body, the rest of it, in the doorway of his bedroom. He turned to Andy and whispered his name.

"Hunh? Yeah?"

Moses moved to his right and pointed at the doorway.

"What the h...Who the fuck is that?"

Moses shrugged.

Everyone looked towards Moses.

"Is that what I think it is?" Reed asked.

Andy took a step toward the bedroom door. "This is what infrasounds do to a human. Pretty much all animal life ends up this way, I guess. We know a dog does."

"We better get to the shop," Moses said.

"You think there's more?"

"Unless there's one in the kitchen," he flicked on the bedroom light and peeked in the doorway, "this is the only one in here, and they usually come in pairs."

"Whose they?" Kip asked.

"Government. Doesn't matter what branch. Always two. At least."

As they headed out the backdoor, past Arabella's web, Jointer blurted, "That's a fuckin' big ass web. What's it doing there?"

"A friend use to live there," Andy said solemnly.

In the backyard, between the house and the shop, on the path to the shop door, they found the remains of another stranger. Government agents, according to Moses. Either that or well dressed thieves. They found no one in the shop.

Moses sat down at the monitor for his plane, Andy and the band crowded in behind to watch.

"Infrared?" Thorton asked as the screen lit up.

Moses nodded, then pushed a key and the scene on the monitor bounced with the motion of the moving model plane as it taxied for take-off from the roof of the shop. A moment later the lighter foreground vanished as the little plane lifted into the air. Moses eyes shifted to the display at the bottom of the screen. Flying by instrument, he leveled the aircraft off at four hundred feet.

"How are you steering it?" Thorton asked as he stepped closer to Moses.

"Joystick," Moses said as he leaned away from the keyboard to allow

Thorton to see. "There's a transmitter on the roof that's connected to the computer so I can fly from here. I've also got the usual remote control, too." He looked at Thorton. "Want to steer?"

Thorton's face lit up like a little boy's on Christmas morn'. "Love to."

Moses rose from the chair and as he stepped away, he pointed to the vertical lines and pointer at the bottom of the screen, "That's the target finder. Keep the pointer on it as much as possible." He pointed to another display on the screen. "That's your flight level there. Altitude is there. In the direction it's going that height will be safe."

"Gotcha," Thorton stated as he plopped into the chair.

As Thorton steered the model plane over the desert, Andy and Z spoke quietly several feet behind the rest.

"What's the plan when you find whoever is behind this?" Z queried.

"Stop him," Andy said flatly. "Anyway I can," he added with conviction, placing his right hand over the bullet wound.

"I still don't understand why you're involved," Z said as Moses approached them. "How come you know about this, anyway?"

Andy looked past Z and out the window to the house. He could see the back door, knowing Arabella's web was just to the right, visions of her running through his mind. "Let's just say I have visions," Andy said dryly.

Z looked back over his shoulder, through the window to the house. He remembered the web and the dead spider. He turned back to Andy. "That the spider that talked to you?"

Andy was obviously stunned at Z's deductive powers, nodding confirmation. "In dreams." He wasn't going to tell anyone about Tabitha. "And always ambiguous. I have a hard time figuring out what she means."

"I can understand why," Z said, a slight sarcasm present in his tone.

"The Spider Spirit is strong in Andy," Moses interjected. "I have spoken with my grandfather at great lengths of what Andy has told me of his dreams. We are on the right path. This man and his machine has to be stopped."

"She found me on the road on my way here," Andy defended. "And if I hadn't lost my truck, I wouldn't be here now."

"You think she talked somebody into stealing your truck?"

"At this point, Z, I'd believe just about anything." Andy looked over at the cot. He was tired, but they could find the source of the infrasounds any minute.

"What if this guy is using a satellite?" Reed asked the room.

"He's not using an uplink," Moses offered.

"Why not?"

"It'd be too risky. He'd be exposed," Moses explained. "Traceable. I just don't think he'd do it."

"What do you think they were looking for?" Andy asked Moses.

"Who? Those two back there?"

Andy nodded.

"How the hell am I suppose to know? Maybe it's you they're concerned about. You're the Gypsy."

"You're the minority."

"You're the long haired hippy."

"Boys. Boys," Z interrupted. "They were watching you at the nightclub."

Andy and Moses stared dumbfounded at Z. Then, in unison, they said, "Beatty."

"We have to find this guy." Andy put a fist to his mouth to cover a yawn. "Before they do."

"Since we're asking questions," Jointer said without looking from the computer screen. "How do we know this guy isn't going to turn this thing back on and puddify us?"

"So far he hasn't hit the same place twice," Andy said.

"That's not much reassurance," Z said as he returned to watch the monitor.

"It's all we got," Moses stated. He looked at Andy, then put a hand on his shoulder. "Why don't you go lay down? I'll wake you as soon as something happens."

"Do I look that tired?"

"You look dead on your feet."

"Thanks. I feel about the same."

As he laid in the shadows, arm draped over his eyes and the voices of the others intruding, he remembered Arabella. She was in his thoughts as he slipped into sleep.

Andy sat cross-legged on a dirt floor facing a hot fire. Beyond the fire was a draped doorway. He had the distinct feeling he was facing East, making him the guest. A low, nearly inaudible drum beat was slowly drifting through the cave. Arabella was here, somewhere. He could feel her. He pulled his eyes from the fire and scanned his surroundings. The walls came into focus as his eyes adjusted. He was in a hogan. The pintings on the walls similar to the cave from a previous vision. He was certain it was Arabella's home. He looked to the ceiling, searching for her web.

There, encircling a small opening in the center, was an orb web. The smoke from the fire escaping through it in wisps. Arabella materialized, then descended from a dense area of strands to Andy's right.

As Arabella dropped from the web on a dragline, her size increased logarithmically until she touched the ground. She was quite larger than Andy. Any bigger and they wouldn't fit inside the room. Her posture looked awkward and uncomfortable, as if she could tip over backwards with the slightest provocation. The dragline was still attached, though, and she looked to be sitting on it, using it for balance.

The little dust she had kicked up was drawn into the updraft of the fire, igniting into sparkles of blue, green, red, and orange. The smoke swirled into wisps of cobwebs, riding the currents up. Arabella turned her face, and fangs, to Andy.

"What will happen if I don't stop this man?" he asked her.

"I do not know what will happen. No one can see tomorrow. It is dynamic. Volatile. Metamorphic. But you must stop him, Andrew," she stated coldly. *"He doth not know what he dwells in."* Then, quietly, in a whisper she added, *"So few of you do."*

"How am I suppose to stop him? I don't even know who it is."

Arabella snapped her head to her left, away from Andy. "I showed you when we first met," she said as if hurt by him not realizing this, then flicked some more dust into the fire. The dust burst into sparkles of colored flame and Arabella was gone. So too, was the hogan.

Andy opened his eyes to the dull image of Kip shaking him. "We found it," Kip said when he saw Andy's eyes open.

Moments later Andy leaned into Moses' view, looking closely at the scene on the monitor. "I've seen that place before," Andy said.

"I know where it is," Moses said. "It's an old, abandoned, missile silo. That's the radio tower there. The silo is off to the left of the screen."

Andy looked to the keyboard and touched a key, then looked at the screen. The camera was moving to the left, and too, the view. The place definitely looked familiar: The fence, the metal tower, the silo doors as they came into view. In the background Andy could see a small building. Linus. The puppet had said something about the place being a secret.

Andy shuddered. This was too weird. This is the place he had seen in that first vision. He had been in this guy's truck. Sat less than a two feet from this madman. And either in his truck or the rest area, is where he picked up Arabella.

"I know who it is," Andy said to the monitor.

"Who?"

"The man that gave me that short lift back in Wyoming," Andy looked at Moses. "Right before I met these guys." Andy pointed a thumb at Glass Reality, then turned back to the screen. "How long will it take us to get there?"

Moses shrugged, his eyes rolling to the ceiling. "Mmm-m-m, 'bout half an hour." He twisted the chair to face Andy. "Maybe an hour. It's down in a flat rimmed by mountains. I think I remember the way in. I haven't been there in over ten years."

"How come you think this asshole driver is our man?" Jointer asked. He was laying on his side on a workbench, head resting on bent arm.

"Arabella told me. When I first met her. I bet she was in his truck when he stopped to pick me up." Andy looked up to Moses and asked, "Do you think she made him stop for me?"

Moses only shrugged. "She's your spider."

Kip turned to Thorton and asked, "Who's Arabella?"

Chapter XII

It was several hours until sunrise. Z had joined Andy and Moses when they left for the missile silo, each armed with large bore pistols that belonged to Moses. In the back seat beside Z, sat a small satchel of explosives.

Z had asked to go along. The rest of Glass Reality stayed at Moses'. They were going to monitor the news and fly the plane home.

Thirty-minutes later the three men were silent as they bucked the ruts of the road that wound down a ridge wall, Z keeping steady pressure on the duffle bag beside him with his hand. The going was slow and bumpy, Moses having to shift into first several times to get through gullies in the tracks. Andy braced his feet on the floorboards and held on to the frame of the jeep as he watched the headlights bring the next bump into sight. His side was starting to ache with a dull sting.

A rough ten minutes later they reached the flat and clipped along at a dusty twenty miles an hour to the center of the basin. The basin, twenty miles wide, was encircled with jagged mountains. The flat floor was still and silent; tests of the infrasound machine killing all life in the basin. The silo was only several miles away.

Moses shut off the headlights when they first saw the radio tower. The moon was bright in the cloudless sky, creating silhouettes to populate the land. The low vegetation spread out into a lazy obstacle course. There was enough light for Moses to drive.

A hundred yards from the tower, the coarse sand crunching like dry cereal beneath the tires, Moses stopped and turned the engine off. The air, cold enough to expose their breath, was fresh and brisk. The radio tower and the fence ahead was the only thing visible. The entrance to below was hidden in distance and darkness. Andy stepped out of the jeep and the sand crackled beneath his shoe with a sharp echo.

Twenty feet from the chain link fence, the small building in clear view, they squatted behind a group of thin bushes, Z behind but between Andy and Moses.

"This place use to have motion and heat sensors all around the perimeter when the government owned it," Moses whispered.

"Let's hope the fence is all this guy has now," Andy whispered back.

Moses studied the compound, then said, "You think anybody's home?"

"I don't see any cars."

"Only one way to find out."

"Wish I had a joint," Z informed anyone listening as he turned away to retrieve the plane.

"How much of that stuff do you smoke?" Moses questioned.

Z turned towards Moses. "Sometimes I think too much, at others, not enough."

Andy scanned the horizon and hillsides for headlights as he and Moses approached the fence, Z heading for the plane a few yards away.

At the fence, Moses reached into the duffle bag and pulled out a pair of wire-cutters. He started cutting a hole in the fence as Andy stood close by, still watching for headlights.

As Moses cut the final strands, Z returned with plane. Moses laid the cut section of fence down before informing Z, "There's another battery for it in the bag. Change it so they can fly it home."

      *   *   *

As the plane headed home, the three ducked through the hole in the fence and headed for the shack. "What does, 'Z', stand for, Z?" Moses asked when they were a few steps from the fence.

Z sighed. "My name's Zacharia Zift. I never liked it. And I always thought of 'Zach' as a cartoon noise. So, ever since about tenth grade, I've called myself Z."

"Hmph," Andy grunted to himself. "I've always thought of Zacharia as an intellectual name, like Leonardo." He said 'Leonardo' with a rough, Italian accent. "Johnathon's a good one, too. So is Sebastion."

"What about Albert, as in Einstein?" Moses tossed in.

"Nah." Andy turned to Moses. "Without the Einstein, the Albert ain't squat," he explained. He then felt a pair of eyes glaring into him. Unable to see more than a dark, grey silhouette of either men from the gibbous moon, Andy knew it was Z and that it was time to drop the subject.

Moments later they were at the lone building. The door to the shack was locked. Moses removed a pry bar from the duffle bag, handed the bag to Andy, then forced the lock. The door opened outward, exposing a dark, musty room.

"Gotta flashlight in that bag?" Z asked.

"I hope so."

"There is."

Andy rummaged through the bag. A moment later he withdrew a small, metal-cased flashlight. "Just the one?"

"I only had two good batteries."

Andy twisted it on. The piercing beam of light splashed on the far wall, dust particles and tiny bugs dancing in the glow. Andy swung the beam around the small room. A staircase leading down was on the wall to their right. "Looks like it's all downhill from here," he quipped.

"Couldn't we just drop the grenades down there," Z pointed to the dark hole of the stairs, "and then run like hell?"

Andy paused, contemplating the idea. He touched his left side, the gunshot wound still a bit tender. He did not want to be shot again, nor did he want to just drop the grenades and run. He wanted to place the grenades inside the machinery that was making the infrasounds. Make sure it was destroyed. But before Andy could reply to Z's proposition, Moses answered for him.

"We should sit down there and wait for this guy to return. Then blow him and his shit up." Moses looked at Andy. "Make sure nobody can do this again."

"Wait. Didn't Reed say that the French have this knowledge?" Andy asked.

"Yeah, but he also said they never put it to use," Z reminded him. "They couldn't get a handle on it. Obviously this guy did. He needs to be stopped, Andy. We have to stop him."

Andy moved the beam of light to Z's chest, keeping it out of his eyes. Z's face lit up with shadows like a child's on Halloween. "When did you get so gung ho?"

Z shrugged. "You could say I'm sick of other people fucking up the world for the rest of us; for whatever reasons they do it."

"Let's see who's home," Moses suggested.

"This guy has got to have lights," Z stated. "Where's the switch?"

"No," Andy snipped. "We don't want him to know we're here. The lights stay off," Andy ordered as he reached the top of the stairs. "It can't be much further."

"He'll know when he sees the door."

"It'll be too late by then." Andy turned and started down the stairs, his metallic footfalls dropping into the black below. Moses and Z followed on either side, one step back.

The staircase hugged the wall down into the darkness. The block wall absorbed the glow of the flashlight, the steps and railing the only things to focus on. The darkness seemed infinite in depth, the stairway an anomaly in the emptiness, the only tangible thing in the darkness.

Z reached out and slid a hand on the railing as they descended. It made him feel just a bit more secure. Moses had his attention focused on the lighted steps, again concerned about just how many of them there were, and if they were down there now. Andy unconsciously moved closer to the wall, confirming its existence.

They walked down another flight of stairs before coming to a metal door. "Told you it wasn't much further." Andy tried the handle and the door opened. He stepped into the room and shined the light on the wall and looked around.

The room was round and deep. The walls poured concrete. A narrow walkway wrapped around the wall and a spiral staircase descended down the middle. A support pole in the center of the staircase broke the flashlight beam on an otherwise seamless wall. He found the light switch on his left just before making a complete circle with the flashlight. "Um, more stairs, guys."

Andy leaned against the railing next to the switch and pointed the light onto the doorway. "Come on in."

When Moses and Z had squeezed by him, Andy pulled the door shut and pushed up the light switch. The black dimmed to a dirty shade of yellow, revealing a cylinder of a room going down, way down. The weak lights, four on either side, were embedded flush in the walls twenty feet apart, shadows and silhouettes linking the darkness across the stairs.

Z leaned over the center railing. "Looks like there's at least two more levels." He straightened and turned to his companions, "I can see a couple crosswalks heading off from the steps and part of another walkway like we're on."

"That would be our first stop," Moses said.

Andy turned to Z. "Lead the way."

Z headed down the steps, the spiral tight and steep. Moses and Andy were two steps behind. Minutes later they were at the next doorway down. It was metal with rivet heads the size of a pea. Z tried the door. It was locked.

"Now what?" Z asked.

"Blow it," Andy said.

"What?!" Moses exclaimed, the single word echoing up and down the shaft.

"Put a grenade next to the door and pull the pin," Andy calmly explained.

"I thought you didn't want them to know we're here?" Moses questioned.

"It's just the one guy. And his control room is behind that door." Andy spoke quietly but firmly.

"How do you know that?" Z asked.

Andy only shrugged. He just knew.

"It's gonna make one helluva noise," Moses stated.

"Put your fingers in your ears," Andy directed.

"Maybe we should check the next level down before doing anything?" Moses stated. "Just to make sure."

The three men gazed back and forth at each other for several moments before Z said, "Let's just blow this door and whatever's inside and get the hell out of here. This place is starting to make my skin crawl."

"Moses is right. We should make sure of what's all here. Make sure we get everything."

*   *   *

The next level down they found a simple wooden door. Vent slats at the top and bottom allowed for convection circulation. A simple knob, no lock. No dead bolt.

It opened up into a long bedroom/living room combination; the bed was at the back of the room, the sofa just off to the left. A coffee table, scattered with books, blocked a straight walk to the bed. A chest-of-drawers helped the illusion of two rooms.

It was as they were leaving the living quarters that they noticed another door, off to the right. This door, too, was as simple as the other, the slats further apart though. There was a cleaner smell, fresher air, coming from behind this door. It was very distinct and noticeable. Z opened the door to an underground greenhouse.

They discovered vegetables and herbs as the walked the length of the room to the far door, encountering flies, gnats, spiders, and bees. The far door opened into a spiral staircase, down the only direction. Moses led the way as the discovered more levels. A hemp garden was the next level down, then a kitchen; with an attached cellar where it stays a constant, cool, thirty-eight degrees. On the bottom level, with a tunnel to the main staircase, was a generator using products from both gardens. A workshop/laboratory was accessed through this tunnel or the main staircase.

On the second level from the bottom, they found a den. The walls of the den were lined with bookshelves, full bookshelves. At the far end was a flat, metal desk. A long table on either wall just in front of it. The three of them spread out along the bookshelves.

"This guy has been down here a long time," Moses said, each one staring at a different section of shelves.

"There's a couple books here dealing with underground engineering," Andy said.

"These over here are about philosophy," Z said. "Plato, Socrates,

Machiavelli, Voltaire."

"Indoor gardening, alchemy, acoustics," Moses listed as he scanned the books he passed. "Computer programming, physics."

"Smart man," Andy deduced.

"Only if he read them all," Moses challenged.

"And understood them," Z countered.

"Smart enough to use infrasounds and not kill himself," Andy finalized.

"Hey," Moses demanded their attention. "Have either of you seen anything on religion?"

"No," came the chorused reply.

Andy spotted an open book on the desk and went to investigate. As he rounded the corner of the desk, he saw that it was a journal. He leaned over it, reading. The author had just turned the page. There was only one entry:

```
11 Dec 0020 hrs:
    In a few minutes Dreamland will become lifeless. My
only concern is getting in and out before the authorities
arrive. I don't foresee any problems, but will need to
stay alert. If only I had more time to get behind the
locked doors.
    LG
```

More time? The eleventh? That's tomorrow. Today. How much time do they have? "Hey, guys..?" Andy skimmed through the pages as he waited for an answer. He glanced at six pages, the images, drawings, and schematics precise. Entries and notes were legible and easy to read. "Hey, guys..?" He closed the book before scooping it up and heading towards his friends. "I think we should get things done and get of here. Our time is limited."

"What did you find?" Moses asked.

"His fuckin' journal. He's ripping off Area 51."

"Bullshit."

"Would I make something like that up? This guys a lunatic!"

"Got some balls on him, too," Moses amazed. "Hitting the government like that. Then, waltzing in there and taking what he wants."

"He's a fruitcake. But hell, if he wasn't doing this, he'd be a politician somewhere." Andy held out the journal, "This thing is almost full. It also says volume nine on the first page."

"So?"

"From just glancing through it, it has drawings, schematics, rants, ravings, diary entries. It has everything that goes through this guys head, except recipes and sex."

"You a speed reader?" quipped Z.

Andy tossed him the journal. "Don't need to be."

Moses stepped over to Z and looked over Z's right shoulder at the markings on the pages. Several moments and countless pages later Moses blurted. "We gotta go."

"Duh," came Andy's reply.

The journal fell to the floor as the men left the room with a purpose in their stride. They quickly climbed the stairs to the control room floor. As they climbed, each would take a moment to catch their breath and offer a plan.

"Let's just blow the door, then the room. No look, just throw. Then, from the top step, drop all the rest and run like hell."

"Fuck the door and the room. Let's drop it all from the top."

"We'll blow the door, and wait. We have to stop him."

"We'll wait for him upstairs."

"We stop him, here." Andy stopped by the locked metal door and knelt down. "We can have everything set by the time he gets back. He won't know anything's wrong 'til it's too late."

"What if he's close and hears the blast?"

Andy placed an explosive charge by the door. "Are you serious? He couldn't hear it if he was right on top of us." He hit the timer. They had ten seconds.

Frequency Seven

Moses and Z headed up the flights, Andy went down.

Chapter XIII

The blast lit the entire shaft, rattling the stairs and reverberating through the walls. On the surface, just as he stepped out of his pickup truck, Linus Greene felt the ground tremble beneath his feet. Instantly he thought, "Someone's inside." He hadn't seen Moses' jeep parked outside the fence. He hadn't seen the hole cut in the fence. But he knew someone was below, inside his home. He leaned back into the truck and opened the glove box. From inside it he pulled a .45 automatic pistol, then headed for the shack. He did not see the two dark, green SUV's bouncing down the rutted road of the cliff behind him.

*   *   *

When the smoke cleared, the three men entered the room. The first through the door, Moses, found the light switch and pushed the little lever up. The room, twenty by thirty feet, flickered into a white, fluorescent glow. It was nearly empty; a long, wooden table stood against the wall on the right, a metal desk against the wall on the left, and some type of control panel lined the far wall from floor to ceiling. The control panel had gauges, dials, a monitor, numerous lights and LED's, switches, and knobs. It appeared to be off. On the table was a mess of papers and spiral notebooks. On the desk was a closed laptop computer. A metal frame desk chair with casters was near the control panel, on the desk side. Moses strolled over to the table and started sifting through the heap of papers. Z went over to the desk, opened the laptop and turned it on. Andy headed straight for the control panel, knowing what it controlled before reaching it - the whispers of Hell. He studied it for several moments before announcing, "This is it."

"You're sure?" Moses asked, dropping the papers in his hands and walking over to Andy. Z remained at the desk, scanning the computer screen, oblivious to the other two.

Before Moses reached Andy, Andy found the power switch and turned the equipment on. There was a hum of electricity as the light for the room dimmed for a moment, then dials and gauges moved, lights and LED's came on, and the monitor flickered on to a view of the silo doors outside.

"Hey, what did you do?" Z demanded from the desk.

"Why?"

"The computer went into a program on its own. It's spitting out a crap load of numbers."

"It's displaying coordinates, frequencies, and amplitudes."

Andy, Z and Moses turned in unison to the strange voice from the doorway. Standing just inside the room was a husky man with short, black hair. Wire-rimmed eyeglasses rested on a long nose. He had a full beard, wore a light jacket over a white shirt with thin green stripes, khaki pants and tennis shoes. In his right hand was a pistol, large bore.

"I would appreciate it if you all would drop whatever weapons you're carrying and step to the middle of the room," the stranger ordered.

As the three men placed their weapons on the desk, Moses asked the obvious, "Who are you?"

"Name's Linus Greene. This is my home you've broken into. Now, just who the fuck are you?"

"The door was open," Z stated.

A gunshot rang out, echoing off the concrete walls, amplifying the sound. The projectile ricocheted off the floor and embedded in the bottom of the table to the trio's left. The three men jumped at once.

"WHO THE HELL ARE YOU AND WHAT THE FUCK ARE YOU DOING IN MY HOME?!" Linus demanded.

Andy recognized him. He was that short ride in Wyoming. He was the guy that shot him. Suddenly he wanted to lunge at him. The gun in Linus' hand, though, caused hesitation.

"I'm Andy," he started, then nodded to his right. "This is Z, that's Moses."

"You with the CIA?"

The three glanced at each other, then Andy said, "No."

"NSA?"

"No."

"Air Force?"

"We're just, civilians," Moses interrupted.

"I'm a musician," Z corrected.

"SHUT UP!"

Andy looked to the floor, slowly raising his head as he coldly said, "We're here to stop you."

There was a pause as a slow smile spread across Linus' face. "Stop me from doing what?"

Andy took one step forward. "From killing people with sound. Like you did in Beatty."

Linus stood his ground, amazed they knew, but too arrogant to deny it. "What do you care? You didn't know 'em."

"I'm the one you shot point blank."

"No shit." Linus studied Andy for just moment. "You did make it. Well, good for you."

"You've killed hundreds of people. You've committed mass murder."

"Phfft! Sandmites. Peasants" He shrugged. "So I'll call myself a nation of one, my machine my army, and I'm at war. Now they're all terrorists, insurgents, rebels, collateral damage," he waved a hand through the air as if to dismiss it all, then leaned towards Andy and snarled, "the enemy. There. Does that make it easier to swallow?"

"What a bunch of bullshit," Z said.

Instantly the barrel belched out a flash, then the crack of a small explosion. Moses jolted back and to his left, the bullet hitting just to the left of his heart. He was dead before he hit the floor. The gun barrel exploded again, this time dropping Z with the back of his head blown away, the bullet having entered through his nose. The third shot hit Andy in the gut at the same level as the first gunshot, but further in, severing an artery. Andy fell to his knees, then over Z.

Linus fired another shot into Andy that grazed his left side, just above the waist, and buried itself into the already dead Z. Andy flinched, unwilling giving the Linus the false impression that he had hit his target. Linus paused several more seconds, scanning the room for any damage.

Things were turned on, but nothing toyed with. He looked to the three corpses on the floor. He felt the need to vomit and rushed from the room.

Andy pushed himself off of Z, pausing to stare at the surprise on Z's face. Moses lay face down, head turned the other way. He was too weak to crawl over to check. Instead, he used the last of his energy to crawl up the desk.

Face to the monitor, Andy read the screen. It was GUI. This controlled the panel, which controlled the sounds. With effort he got his hand on the mouse and opened properties. He wasn't sure what he was doing, but he was sure he had to stop Linus. He was sure he wanted revenge. Moses was like a brother. Z becoming a good friend. And, he was sure he was dying. He checked the surround sound box, maximized the volume, turned "Direction Control" to off, then clicked start.

    Andy more dropped than slid back to the floor. Before drifting off into a loss of blood sleep, he felt the breeze of the infrasound waves begin to emanate.

    The frequency was seven hertz. The amplitude was sufficient enough to carry the signal around and through the globe. They traveled through the air at around seven hundred fifty miles per hour. Andy was already dead when the infrasounds ravaged his body and the bodies of his dead friends. Linus Greene exploded more than anything else, death instantaneous. The five men in suits descending the spiral staircase collapsed and dripped through the metal-mesh decking. The man left to watch the vehicles melted were he stood.

    Along the surface of the ground, and down and through the planet, the sound waves sped along at anywhere from three thousand to ten thousand miles per hour.

    Reed, Thorton, Kip and Jointer collapsed where they were, standing or sitting, to quivering lumps on the floor.

    Grey Eagle, sitting in the hogan, eyes closed, finishing off the batch he had shared with Andy and his grandson, converses with his sister before collapsing into a pool of loose skin. Minutes later Andy's grandparents died in their sleep.

    Death moved in concentric rings around the Frequency Seven machine. Those within twenty miles actually heard the sounds. A deep bass that rattled their eyes and shattered windows. The road block, people in their cars, coyotes and rabbits, birds, snakes, elephants, everything was turned into an amorphous glob of pudding. Within hours, all animal life around the globe succumbed in succession to the infrasounds in order of distance from the source and the material beneath their feet.

    *   *   *

Frequency Seven

On an island in the southern Indian Ocean, two teenagers survived the apocalypse. They were in coconut trees, hunting for a late afternoon snack. The island was a French possession, the Isle Amsterdam. By the time the air borne infrasounds reached them, they were too weak to do anything but give the two a short tingle. These two were to be the new Adam and Eve. But for the near future, plants and insects suddenly rule the world.

Chapter XIV

Andy sat on a web, the strands as thick as a ships mooring line, feet dangling above the Earth below. A vibration told him Arabella was approaching. He continued to stare at the blue orb below until the spider was beside him. When he spoke to her, he didn't look up. "I thought I was suppose to save the world."

"You did."

"What!? I failed. Everything's. . .dead. They won't be telling any stories about me now."

"Not everything is dead. The world will grow again. Life will rejuvenate."

Andy looked at Arabella, a harsh expression, a mixture of deep sorrow and rage. "My best killed everyone on the planet. How could you let this happen?"

"I have no control over what happens. Man was certain to destroy the planet. Only it was believed to have been done with nuclear weapons, which would have killed everything. The planet itself would have been dead. No life would have been able to live on it. Except cockroaches. Man, the most intelligent thing on the planet, and he designs a weapon that will kill everything except cockroaches. Kind of makes you wonder about the most intelligent part."

"What the hell is that suppose to mean?"

She did a four legged shrug. "Nothing, I suppose. I have nothing against cockroaches. Personally."

"What?"

"Man has always thought himself above nature. Better than nature. Man has been destroying his home, little by little, for centuries. Dirtying the water, poisoning the soil and clouding the air with deadly chemicals. Then he came up with nuclear power. It was only a matter of time before he destroyed the very planet that gave him life. At least this way, there is still plant life. There are still insects and microbes. In time, animal life will resume. Perhaps this time, however, if there is such a creature as Man, he will respect the Mother."

Then a child's voice, sweet and feminine, spoke, "Everything's going to be fine."